Alan Hunter was born in Hoveton, Norfolk in 1922. He left school at the age of fourteen to work on his father's farm, spending his spare time sailing on the Norfolk Broads and writing nature notes for the *Eastern Evening News*. He also wrote poetry, some of which was published while he was in the RAF during the Second World War. By 1950, he was running his own bookshop in Norwich. In 1955, the first of what would become a series of forty-six George Gently novels was published. He died in 2005, aged eighty-two.

The Inspector George Gently series

Gently Where She Lay

Alan Hunter

Constable & Robinson Ltd
55–56 Russell Square
London WC1B 4HP
www.constablerobinson.com

First published in the UK by Cassell & Company Ltd., 1972

This paperback edition published by C&R Crime,
an imprint of Constable & Robinson Ltd., 2013

A copy of the British Library Cataloguing in Publication
Data is available from the British Library.

ISBN 978-1-47210-869-2 (paperback)
ISBN 978-1-47210-877-7 (ebook)

Typeset by TW Typesetting, Plymouth, Devon

Printed and bound by CPI Group (UK) Ltd, Croydon, CR0 YY

1 3 5 7 9 10 8 6 4 2

CHAPTER ONE

I LOCKED THE door of the cottage, Seacrest, where only policemen had entered since Tuesday, and stood looking at the green in front of it and at the evening sea behind white-painted railings. This was the view Vivienne Selly had seen every time she had stepped through her door: the small, trim green with its three flower-beds, the cottage opposite, and the sea below. Cars passed by her window, coming from the town and turning sharp left to join the promenade; strollers idled along the cliff-top footway, or rested on one of the two green benches. But it was the sea that dominated the scene, spreading high and wide below the cliff. In her upstairs sitting-room Vivienne had placed a chair from which you could see the sea and nothing else. It was like being in a ship, sitting up there, with the great wrinkled plain moving at your elbow: looking down on seabirds winging across the wave-crests, or a long-shore fishing-boat plugging towards the harbour. But then the sea would have been special to Vivienne, who'd come from a poor neighbourhood in Birmingham. She'd have thought it heaven, two years ago, when the Sellys moved to Wolmering from Smethwick.

I slipped the key in my pocket and strolled over the grass to the footway and railings. Opposite the little green steps descended the cliff, which was neither high nor remarkably steep. But the view was surprising. Southwards, to my right, was an irregular line of fine Georgian houses (echoing a lovely house with rococo bows, a few doors up from the Selly cottage); then the cliff-top swelled greenly, with a hint of distant houses, and beyond stretched the semicircle of a huge, cliffy bay. The cliffs there were steep and of a honey-cake colour. They were helmed partly with dark woods and, further off, a heathery heath. At the bay's most distant point, say six or seven miles off, the bluish cube of an atomic power-station notched mistily in the dulled sky. Northwards the view was less exciting, being mostly of the promenade and a prosaic pier, but still extensive, and prettily framed by tilted fields and receding cliffs. And all of it, north and south, was just twenty steps from Vivienne's door. Wouldn't it have consoled her on those dull days when Selly was away on his travels?

I shook my head and turned along the footway, which we knew had been her route on the Tuesday evening. At about this hour, eight p.m., she had locked her door for the last time. She had been nicely dressed – we had her clothes. The key she had used was the one in my pocket. She had taken her handbag, which contained a little money and the medical card by which she'd been identified. Nothing was abnormal. As far as we knew she had simply set out for an evening stroll, perhaps intending to have a drink later at the Pelican where (according to the barman) she was an occasional customer. What had been different about Tuesday? Whose eye had been on her as she set out, looking neat and pretty in a midi frock of a delicate beige that had probably flattered her pale complexion?

The footway was narrow. It passed under the windows of a number of charming, sea-facing cottages, some of which had miniature gardens with little bits of sculpture let in beside them. Expensive, of course. Wolmering is where the gently affluent retire; these small but immaculate period-dwellings would change hands like rare paintings. Inspector Eyke had made his rounds here. None of the residents remembered seeing Vivienne. No doubt in these parlours one's eye caught the habit of gliding unimpressed over the passers in the footway, and in fact, at the same time of the evening, I peered into one empty room after another. Were the inmates all at dinner in rear-facing dining-rooms? The parlours might almost have been there for show. But however it was, I passed unobserved: as Vivienne Selly had done before me.

The cottages terminated and I came to a chapel-like building with a sign-board inscribed: The Fisherman's Rest Room. A dusty model of a beach-yawl occupied one of its windows, through which I could also see the face of a large wall-dock. The place was closed, but two elderly fishermen were seated on a bench outside. They glanced at me casually. One was smoking his pipe, the other had an evening paper in his hand. I paused in front of them.

'Police. I wonder if you'd mind answering a couple of questions?'

They talked with that sing-song local accent that seems to take you at once into its confidence but which, nevertheless, is never far from quiet irony. The pipe-smoker's name was Bob Lockett and his mate's George Duffield. They must have known I wasn't a local policeman but they didn't question my credentials. But they couldn't help me. On Tuesday evening they'd been down at the net-store, at the harbour. Would they have known Mrs Selly by sight? Bob Lockett would. For just a moment, his eye held a gleam.

I left them. Next to the Rest Room was a cul-de-sac, reaching down from the town. It was filled with cars on both sides and there was a pub a few yards along it. The cars were deserted. Higher up, some youths and girls stood round a scooter, and a couple (they looked like visitors) were staring in the window of a tackle-shop. Nothing for me: though I made automatic note of the numbers of the two cars parked next to the footway.

Now, as I turned the corner by the cul-de-sac, I was coming to the aristocratic quarter. Behind long, narrow gardens, expensively maintained, ranged the terrace of majestic Georgian villas. The terrace was a medley: each spacious house had been allowed to follow its own genius; but the almost irresponsible good taste of Georgian builders had ensured that the group was in accord with itself. I lingered to admire it . . . had Vivienne done the same? Here the footway was an isolated stretch between corners. Below, without access, ran a lower promenade, on which were set beach-huts in a marshalled row. The footway was visible from both villas and promenade but neither had an uninterrupted view; shrubs, low walls and distance obscured it from the former; foreshortening and tamarisk scrub from watchers below. The section, to a certain extent, was secluded . . . what happened here might pass unseen.

But Vivienne had passed this point safely: according to our witness, Mrs Lake. Mrs Lake had reported meeting her 'up at the Guns', estimating the time at eight-fifteen. Had Vivienne returned this way? Nobody could tell us. Mrs Lake's was the only sighting . . . and I, how many people had I met, following the same route at the same time?

I walked on. Just around the next corner the footway widened into an open space. Here the council had erected a wooden shelter: and it was at the shelter I met the girls.

Four girls.

I had been given only a cursory description of them by Inspector Eyke, but one girl had glowing red hair, which made recognition of the group easy. Three were wearing the deep maroon skirt-and-blazer uniform which distinguished pupils of Huntingfield School, the fourth – she was probably the day-girl, Pamela Rede – a blue maxi dress, beneath which one could see her bare feet. They were standing round Pamela and talking earnestly, each in a different, unconscious pose; coltish young girls of eighteen, near the point of becoming women.

They saw me and the talking stopped. They faced me haughtily, eyes alert. At once one was aware of closing defences, of a group solidarity in the face of threat. The sensation was almost tangible, like the sudden creation of an electric field, and as I approached them their poses altered, became more compact, directed towards me. I smiled at the girl in the maxi.

'Miss Pamela Rede?'

She didn't reply. She was a tall, pallid-faced girl with shoulder-length fair hair and slightly protruding green eyes. The red-haired girl was Diane Culpho. The others would be Barbara Mells and Anne Brundish. Sixth-formers. They seemed to masquerade a little in the sex-denial of their uniforms.

'My name is Chief Superintendent Gently. I'm investigating the death of Mrs Selly.'

'We didn't kill her.'

'That wasn't the suggestion!'

'And anyway, the police have seen us already.'

I kept smiling at her. She was trembling slightly in spite of the splendid hauteur of her voice. Her father, I understood from Eyke, was a career-diplomat, currently attached in Buenos Aires. Pamela lived with her uncle, Major Rede, who owned a house overlooking the Common. She'd been born in India; there was an Oriental touch in the long beaten-silver necklace she wore with the maxi.

'You four people are rather important to us. I'm afraid you'll have to put up with our questions.'

'But we told them *everything*.'

'Yes – but I'm fresh to it. Why don't we start with introductions?'

The electric field tensed. This was the moment when the cat could jump either way. I wasn't simple enough to expect them to confide in me but I needed to get them talking, reacting. Pamela's eyes yielded nothing. I turned to give the red-haired girl a grin.

'You'll be Diane, of course. Miss Culpho.'

Another tight pause: then Miss Culpho giggled.

I deliberately lingered over the introductions, putting questions that were only half-relevant. I was testing them, but they were testing me too and deciding just how much they ought to thaw. Pamela was clearly the group's leader. Diane Culpho was their jester. She was slightly plump, but with a pretty rounded face, and her soft hair was almost the colour of poppies. Barbara Mells was a staid-looking girl; she was the daughter of an Eastwich architect. Anne Brundish, from Wimbledon, had tomboy good looks and a big-boned, athletic figure. None of them beauties, though perhaps Diane would shed her plumpness and grow into elegance. Brains were probably shared between Diane and Pamela; the other two would labour for their pass-marks.

Four girls . . . what had drawn them into the orbit of a Vivienne Selly? Average girls: you would have expected them to go thoughtlessly on their appointed ways.

'How long had you known Mrs Selly?'

They looked at each other. 'About a year,' Pamela said flatly.

'Where did you meet her?'

'Oh, one Open Day. We saw her around the tennis courts.'

7

'She spoke to you?'

A shrug. I could feel the ice beginning to form again. Dangerous ground: they guessed what I knew, but they were never going to admit it. I switched my attack.

'I expect you knew her as well as most people in Wolmering. That's why it's important for me to talk to you, to get all the information you can give me. Sometimes the vital fact is a small thing, a detail that seems too vague, too trivial. Like some innocent habit of Mrs Selly's, or a hint about money she expected to receive.' I looked earnestly at each girl. 'Tell me, did you see much of her husband?'

Diane coloured a little: they all gazed at me fixedly.

'Well . . . did you?'

Pamela jingled her necklace. 'Of course we met him once or twice. He was a boor. Viv hated him. It was a big relief when he went away.'

I nodded. 'There were scenes, were there?'

'Oh, Viv didn't give him that satisfaction.'

'Did she tell him she hated him?'

'She told him to get out,' Diane said.

'You were present?'

Diane coloured again, but didn't answer.

'It was about other women,' Anne Brundish said suddenly. 'He was away from home a lot, you know. Commercial traveller and all that. He'd got women all over the place.' She shut up as suddenly, biting her lip.

'I think you know all about that,' Pamela said. 'But he's still in the district – that's important, isn't it? We happen to know he's living in Castleford.'

I smiled at her. 'Is it important?'

Her green eyes jumped at me. 'Of course. Who else would want to get rid of Viv? He was paying her an allowance, wasn't he?'

'But . . . did he hate *her*?'

'Yes – he did hate her! Viv was utterly superior to him.'

'How, Miss Rede?'

'Just – superior! She belonged to a different league.'

She made a swerving movement with her shoulders, setting her necklace dinking again; and the others stared at me intently, as though anxious I should know they seconded the point. Yet in what sense could Vivienne have been 'superior' – a Brummie ex-typist who'd married a rep? It didn't show in her books, her furniture; in the negative life she'd been living at Wolmering.

'I'll bet you haven't talked to him,' Pamela said scornfully. 'It's so obvious, yet you won't do anything.'

'We shall talk to him,' I said. 'We talk to everyone.'

'But—' It was her turn to colour.

'Perhaps you've seen George Selly lately?'

'No.'

'Or perhaps Mrs Selly spoke of him on Tuesday?'

She shook her head. 'But he's a rotter and a liar. You shouldn't put any faith in what he tells you.'

'He's an animal,' Barbara Mells said. 'A male animal.'

'In fact, you don't have a good word for him.'

'Because he did it,' Pamela said. 'We all think so.'

She snatched a look at the others. They nodded approval.

9

* * *

I let them relax while I lit my pipe and while two couples passed along the footway. The sun, coming low from behind the houses, was touching the grey sea with frail light. An aquatint evening. Wolmering was a town that would have attracted the nineteenth-century watercolourists. No doubt if I had leisure to search in the library I would find views by Sandby, Cotman, Prout. From a distance what you'd see would be clustering houses on a promontory lifting towards the sea and supporting a plump, white light-house and the sharp-lined tower of a flint church. It cried for painting: in fact I had seen an artist at work there that afternoon.

I broke the match I'd lit my pipe with and dropped the pieces in a litter-bin. The girls watched. They'd stood quite silent while I went through my little ritual. To them I'd be some sort of stern uncle, a man, and well-stricken in years: a male, but now less of an animal. Certainly beyond understanding them. I blew a smoke-ring.

'Do you sixth-formers get into town when you like?'

They shifted a little, uneasy, wondering where this was going to lead. Diane spoke for them.

'It's not quite like that. We have to get leave to come out.'

'When are you due back?'

'At nine p.m. Pam's going to drive us in her Mini.'

'But you get afternoons off?'

'Well . . . sometimes! Like when there are games and we aren't playing.'

'And that would have been the case on Tuesday?'

She nodded, flushing. Now I'd got to it!

'It was Junior Tennis,' Pamela said quickly. 'Seniors aren't obliged to stay for that. Some of us volunteer to umpire, but we don't have to unless we like.'

'There isn't some . . . alternative programme?'

'All right! There's the Natural History Ramble.'

'But nobody much goes on it,' Diane said, very rosy. 'It's just mostly for a few who are interested.'

I puffed and didn't comment. They must already have been on the mat for this. Since Tuesday's incident there would be a rigorous roll-call for all opting ramblers on games afternoons. Evening leave, I imagined, came in at all times for searching scrutiny; the three boarders were probably out now on an invitation under-written by Pamela's guardians.

'Did Mrs Selly know you were going to visit her?'

'Yes,' Pamela said tightly. 'I gave her a ring.'

'No reluctance on her part?'

'Of course not.'

'We always went on Tuesdays when we could,' Diane said.

'I'd like you to describe this visit to me,' I said. 'Just run through it the way it happened – what time you got there, what mood she was in, what you talked about; anything you can remember.'

They looked at each other, then the three of them at Pamela. Pamela had a sulky, withdrawn expression. She looked past me at the sea, her eyes hooded, as though really she was a very long way away.

'We got there soon after two,' she said. 'And we had to leave again at twenty-past four. Well . . . we talked.

11

I don't know what about. Perhaps Viv was warning us not to talk to strange men.'

'She was discussing men?'

Pamela shrugged. 'Isn't that what women usually talk about? Viv knew about men, how rotten they are. With a husband like hers she should know.'

'But did she mention any specific men?'

Pamela hesitated, shook her head. I looked at the others: they stared back blankly. Diane had a little flush about her neck.

'About her mood then. Did she seem happy?'

'Oh, about the usual,' Pamela said.

'She wasn't depressed?'

'I don't think so.'

'Perhaps extra-talkative.'

'Not that I noticed.'

'Did she mention, for example, that she was looking forward to something – a treat, some money, meeting someone?'

Pamela ran her necklace through her fingers. 'I don't remember that,' she said.

'She did—' Diane began, then stopped to blush. Everyone looked at Diane.

'Yes?'

'Well . . . talking about men! She said it was up to a woman to get all she could out of them.'

I nodded. 'She was just talking about men?'

'Yes . . . you know! It was meant for a joke.'

'But some specific man had been mentioned?'

'No! Well, I thought she was talking about her husband.'

I paused to look round the little group. 'I want to

get this very clear,' I said. 'Did Mrs Selly mention a man, *any* man, while you were there with her on Tuesday afternoon?'

'We've told you,' Pamela said sulkily. 'She didn't.'

'Had she ever mentioned any man of her acquaintance?'

'No.'

'She didn't like men,' Barbara Mells said. Her face was quite blank. The rest were silent.

I let that remark hang in the air while I struck a fresh light for my pipe. It had come out so casually, so unemphatically, yet everyone present knew the weight of it. Would I pick it up? They were holding their breath. Diane was frowning at a spot near her feet. Barbara Mells now had the faintest of smirks, as though she were secretly proud of what she'd said. I puffed a few times then snapped my match.

'Very well. Let's try to take this visit from the beginning. Pamela parked her Mini and you rang the doorbell. What was Mrs Selly wearing when she answered the door?'

They had begun to relax but the question tensed them again. Pamela flicked a look at Barbara Mells.

'Viv wasn't dressed.'

'How do you mean?'

'Well . . . I suppose she'd been having a bath.'

'She was wearing her dressing gown.'

'Yes.'

'The lace one.'

Pamela made a small motion with her shoulders.

'I gave her that,' Diane said defiantly. 'It was a birthday present. She liked wearing it.'

'Viv didn't dress about the house,' Pamela said. 'It was one of her things, that's all.'

I glanced at the other two, but they weren't saying anything. Barbara Mells' expression was mulish. She was a sallow-complexioned girl with lean cheeks and a small colourless mouth.

'Was Mrs Selly pleased to see you?'

'Of course,' Pamela said.

'She welcomed you – laughed, made a fuss?'

'No. Viv wasn't that sort of person.'

'But she was pleased to see you. You went into the hall. She said something like: "Let's go up to the sitting-room." Then you all went up the narrow staircase and turned left into her front room. Who sat on the easy chair facing the window?'

A pause while Pamela fingered her necklace. Then:

'Look, it wasn't like that at all! To start with, we went through to the kitchen first. Viv had the kettle on for a cup of tea.'

'Tea?'

'Yes – tea!'

'And later on, no doubt, you washed up the cups for her?'

'Well, she'd wash up anyway, wouldn't she?'

I shook my head. 'She hadn't washed up anything.'

Pamela jerked the necklace. 'I can't help that! Viv made some tea and we took it upstairs. And it was me who sat in the chair by the window – I wanted to keep an eye on my car.'

I shrugged – who wouldn't? 'Where else did you go besides the kitchen and the sitting-room?'

'Nowhere else.'

'Nowhere?' I looked at the others: they didn't answer. 'So,' I said. 'You stayed in the sitting-room. You were there for a little over two hours. That gave you plenty of time to talk – and this took place only two days ago.'

'We can't remember everything!' Pamela snapped.

'On the contrary, I think you'd've remembered this. Your last conversation with your friend.'

'Perhaps we don't want to tell you,' Barbara Mells said.

I stared at this girl (whom I was beginning to dislike); then suddenly, disgustedly, I turned my back on them. I had promised Eyke I would use kid gloves, but what was that getting me except lies and evasions? These kids weren't innocent, and there was something they could tell me which otherwise we'd have to ferret out by routine: something it was important to know quickly – and I didn't have to live with Wolmering afterwards. I kept staring out to sea.

'Now listen! I've just come from Mrs Selly's cottage. Nothing there has been touched since she left it, and I'm an expert at reading evidence. The sitting-room is neat. The bedroom isn't. That big bed looks as though an army had manoeuvred on it. There are five used glasses on the tallboy, a whisky-decanter and an ashtray spilling butt-ends. And there's a riding whip lying on the bed and some woven nylon rope knotted to the bed-frame. And in the bathroom there are a lot of soiled towels and both it and the bedroom stink like a harem. If some perverted orgy hasn't been going on there then the scene was faked by an expert. So are you still going to tell me you were drinking tea in the sitting-room and holding a long conversation you can't remember?'

I swung back to them. Pamela's eyes were popping; Diane, strawberry-coloured, was staring at her feet. The boy-like Anne Brundish had gone pale and trembly. Only Barbara Mells was still composed, still smirking.

'Well?'

Pamela swallowed. 'All that . . . it could have happened when we weren't there.'

'We shall take your prints,' I said. 'They'll match the prints on the glasses.'

'But we used the glasses,' Barbara Mells said smoothly. 'Viv gave us a soft drink just before we left.'

'And she used them again – without washing them?'

'Oh, Viv wasn't too particular.'

I gave Barbara Mells a hard look: she humped her thin back and lowered her eyes. I could see Diane's hands working. They were balled into fists and pressed to her sides.

'Don't any of you care what happened?' I asked. 'Did Vivienne Selly mean so little to you? It doesn't matter that you can perhaps help us catch the person who took away her life?'

Pamela shivered. 'But we can't help—'

'Yes, you can. You can help me *now*. I want to know if what happened at the cottage had any connection with her death.'

'It wasn't . . . it was nothing . . .'

'How do you know?'

'Well . . . I'm certain.'

'There's only one way you can be certain.'

Pamela rustled her necklace, was silent.

I turned to Diane. Diane flinched; her fists ground tighter into her maroon skirt. But then suddenly she threw back her flaming head and stared at me with fierce blue eyes.

'All right – it was us then! Us who did everything you think. Viv didn't have any truck with other people – and she didn't have a boyfriend, either!'

'Thank you, Miss Culpho.'

She couldn't blush deeper: even her hands were pink and swollen. And the fierceness of her eyes flickered painfully: she looked for a moment lost, very vulnerable.

'This would be the last of a – number – of occasions?'

'Yes. And it would have been the last one anyway.'

'How was that?'

'We'd been shopped.' She half-glanced at Pamela. 'Sweffy knew.'

'Sweffy . . . ?'

'Miss Swefling. Our headmistress at the school. Somebody must have dropped her a hint because she had us on the carpet the same day.'

'When?'

'Oh, oh!' Pamela exclaimed. 'I think you've blabbed enough, Di.'

'When?' I said.

'When we got back. She was waiting when we got in.'

Now she let her eyes sink again, though her feet were planted apart: somehow defiant. But she was waiting for the axe to fall, for the full weight of my punitive authority. Pamela had a drag-mouthed expression, her eyebrows raised as though in distaste. A little extra pressure and she'd probably become hysterical for all her pose of being the spokeswoman. It was Barbara Mells who was the tough one. Quite calmly she was studying *my* expression. Then, wholly casual, she reached for Pamela's wrist and turned it so as to see her wrist-watch.

'I think it's time we were getting back.'

'Wait,' I said. 'I haven't finished.'

'But we mustn't be late. Not after Tuesday.'

'You are helping the police.'

Barbara Mells smirked.

I turned to Diane again. 'So Miss Swefling knew. Who did she say told her?'

'She didn't,' Diane said, not meeting my eyes. 'She just said she was shocked and that we'd have to stop it.'

'She was angry?'

Diane didn't answer.

'She threatened to expel us,' Barbara Mells smirked. 'It was rather funny. It so happens that we leave at the end of this term anyway.'

'She gave us extra duties,' Diane said.

'As though they mattered,' Barbara Mells sneered.

'And she was going to talk to Viv – report her to the police if she didn't stop seeing us.'

I looked at Pamela. 'Were you included in this lecture?'

'Oh yes. I was nabbed before I could drive off. But Sweffy couldn't give me extra duties, could she, and anyway she thinks I'm completely depraved.' She jingled the necklace. 'I'm the cad of the Sixth. I spend my breaks reading Henry Miller.'

'For the rest of the evening – you three were in school?'

'We had to take junior prep,' Diane said.

'And you, Miss Rede?'

'At home, naturally. Junior prep isn't for day girls.'

'You were with your uncle and aunt?'

'Well . . . not all the evening. I went for a spin in the Mini. But I didn't call on Viv, if that's what you're hinting. Not after that splendid lecture by Sweffy.'

'It didn't occur to you to warn her.'

Pamela hesitated. 'Well, I didn't,' she said. 'I went for a run to Maidensmere, and called in at the Half Moon there for a cider.'

'Thank you,' I said. 'That's very definite.'

'It's what you'd call an alibi,' Barbara Mells murmured.

I treated Miss Mells to a second stare and she had the grace to erase her smirk.

'One further point and then you can go. It concerns Mrs Selly's dog. As you probably know, we've been looking for it. Did you see it in her house on Tuesday?'

They exchanged looks as though fearing a trap.

'She kept it in the kitchen,' Anne Brundish said, doubtfully.

'I think I heard it,' Diane said. She flushed directly. 'We didn't go in the kitchen.'

'Did anyone else see it?'

They murmured negatives, perhaps wondering what my interest in the dog could be. It was called Rags, Anne Brundish volunteered, a wire-haired terrier; but they really hadn't noticed it on Tuesday.

19

And so I dismissed them, and they trailed off quietly through a gap that gave access to the Town Green. I watched them cross it: Pamela with Barbara Mells, Anne Brundish tagging close to them, Diane at a distance. Four girls. They reached a red Mini and I heard a spurt of nervous laughter. Then they piled in, all limbs, and gunned the engine and rocketed away.

What more did I know . . . ?

I turned to watch a long-shore boat ploughing its track through the gentle swell. The low sun was lighting the face of its helmsman: yellowing the gulls that sailed in its wake.

CHAPTER TWO

S OME NOTES.
   Vivienne herself. My acquaintance, as usual, was post-surgical. But there were good photographs, and Eyke had summarised a description from statements of witnesses. 5′3″, slim build, dark hair, pale complexion, brown eyes, cleft chin, Midlands accent, age 34.

That's the diagram. Filling it in, she had slightly flattened, Creole-type features, eyebrows slanted, chin pointed, cheekbones high but not prominent. The eyes were dark brown and glittering. The hair, worn shoulder-length, was coarse and straight. She was fine-boned, had long-fingered hands, long limbs and narrow hips; spoke in a low, husky voice as though suffering from a permanent sore throat.

An exotic-looking woman.

None of the photographs showed her smiling.

A typical expression showed half-parted lips and eyes de-focused, faintly ecstatic. (Incipient heart-disease? No mention of this in the P.M. report.)

Asocial: the four girls appeared to have been her only acquaintances. Husband left her about twelve months earlier (coincident perhaps with her meeting the girls). She'd have a drink in the Pelican or one of the other pubs but rarely joined in conversation. Apparently unattractive to men. Not 'on terms' with her neighbours.

Vivienne's dog. The witness Lake couldn't remember if she'd seen it with Vivienne. Granted, witnesses are notorious for blind spots and it may have been with Vivienne just the same. She may have let it off the lead when she reached the Guns (a very likely hypothesis), and then unless she was ostentatiously swinging the lead there would be no indication she had a dog with her. But the dog was missing, and if Vivienne hadn't taken it with her, when and how had it disappeared? This was Thursday evening and no report of it yet.

Conjectures about the dog. If she'd left it at home then someone had released it before ten a.m. on Wednesday (this was the time the police had visited the cottage following identification of the body). Cottage not broken into but the murderer could have used Vivienne's key (object: to remove incriminating evidence? No sign of the cottage having been searched). The key, if used, had been returned to her handbag.

Alternatively: if she'd taken the dog with her and it had escaped the notice of witness: why, supposing the murderer had made away with it, had he bothered to conceal the corpse? It could tell us nothing. He might as well have left it with Vivienne on the Common. (Some imponderable factor here, like the murderer being psychotically affected by dogs?)

Lastly (and unfortunately possible) witness could have mistaken her identification. Meaning we would have no knowledge at all of Vivienne's movements at the critical time on Tuesday evening. This would throw us back to around four p.m., when the girls left the cottage. Very discouraging thought: Eyke now searching for additional witnesses.

I continued to follow the footway. After skirting more houses it dipped abruptly to the lower promenade, where there was a bench and where a few small boats lay higgledy-piggledy on the concrete. A discreet, sea-watching spot. The cliff and the steep paths damped out all land sounds. The bench was niched into the cliff and out of sight of the lower promenade. I prowled around. The boats looked neglected and were dogged with sand and dried seaweed. Somebody had been eating fish-and-chips and had thrust the wrappings into the tamarisks. Somebody else had waited for quite a while to judge from a scatter of matches and cigarette-butts. And somebody else had halted briefly while their dog deposited faeces behind the bench.

Vivienne. . . ?

I smile sourly to myself. Perhaps I should have the faeces dated! Yet there they were, temptingly suggesting a verification were much needed. That the dog *had* been with her, with the added bonus of a reason for Mrs Lake's uncertainty: here, Vivienne had detached the lead in order to proceed with greater dignity. It fitted prettily because the Guns were only just above, on the diff. The dog could have been still about its business when Vivienne encountered witness. Then perhaps the lead or Vivienne's turning her head had half-suggested the presence of a dog to Mrs

23

Lake, though not strongly enough for her to be positive of it when she came to make her statement. Yes: pretty. Only the faeces of a dog are not yet a rarity in the urban scene . . .

So I left them, and went on up the steep, short ascent to the cliff-top, to a suddenly-presented view of the feature known as the Guns. The Guns were no myth. They were a row of six eighteenth-century naval cannon, mounted on massive oak carriages and pointing bravely out to sea. Apparently the Dutch in their naval heyday had once the temerity to bombard Wolmering, in consequence of which these six iron monsters had been stationed on the cliff, to remain there ever after. Impressive monuments. I walked to the nearest and knocked out my pipe on the carriage. Then I climbed astride it, like a kid, and surveyed the spot from which Vivienne had vanished.

It was another example of those greens which gave a distinctive flavour to Wolmering, in this case about an acre of sweet-smelling meadow with a bit of bramble and gorse in the corner. One angle shaded away to the Town Green, with a glimpse of the road and the houses beyond it, but the immediate background was occupied by three fortunate houses which (I had been told) were the most expensive in Wolmering: to the east they faced the sea, to the west the Common and the marshes of the Wolmer river. Eyke had cast his net here but had taken no fish. The largest house, of red brick, was empty. Its two neighbours, one a period cottage, one a crisp modern house in the style of the thirties, were a little hidden by their own shrubs and by the island of bramble and gorse. At the far end of the green, beside a white-painted flag-pole, stood a look-out post belonging to the coastguards, but this had not been manned on Tuesday evening (it appeared empty now). All very charming: but it might have been a stage set, so very lifeless did it seem. The last of the sun was fading from it and the sea's murmur from below was nearly inaudible.

I slid down from the cannon and crossed the footway to lean on the rails guarding the cliff-edge. Below, the beach was composed of large shingle, not very inviting either to strollers or bathers. Nobody there. A long way to the south I could see three figures walking on the sand-dunes, but to the north the beach stretched vacantly till the view was interrupted by the pier. Wolmering was a puzzle. An investigation at a seaside resort is usually bedevilled by an overplus of possible witnesses. Up the coast a bit at Starmouth the beaches and promenades would still be crowded with visitors and trippers. Here there might have been a curfew, or a plague-flag limply hanging from the coastguard's flag-pole. And I didn't think the fact that Vivienne Selly had died was in the least way responsible. No. This was how it was. This was the evening peace of Wolmering. The affluent elderly had settled in their drawing-rooms and left such spots as the Guns to odd peasants like me . . .

I turned from the rails in a moment of sympathy for Eyke: to find I was no longer so conspicuously solitary. A woman had appeared from behind the look-out and was firmly striding towards me. An elderly woman. She was dressed in soft tweed and flourished a stick with a silver knob. I had a flash of premonition: this woman had been spying on me. Then another: she was Mrs Lake. I waited at the rail. She came on briskly, her eyes facing rigidly before her. I stepped forward to intercept her: and found the stick thrusting suddenly at my face.

'Stand back!'

'I beg your pardon!'

'You had better keep your distance, my man.'

I certainly did that! There was nothing tentative in the way the brass ferrule was cocked before my eyes. 'I merely wish to speak to you. Are you Mrs Lake?'

'Yes. But I don't think I know you.'

'I'm a police officer.'

'That's easily said. If you're a policeman, produce your warrant.'

I did produce it. Mrs Lake stared at it, then at me, then again at the card. Finally the ferrule dipped away from my eyes, though the stick was still held handy.

'Well, if that's the case, I'm sorry. But one daren't take chances with strangers up here. I'm hoping I shall spot him, you know. And he won't find me as easy as he did Mrs Selly.'

My turn to stare! 'Do you think that's wise?'

'Oh, I'm not a fool,' Mrs Lake said. 'I wouldn't tackle him. That's not my idea. But perhaps he'll come back here, and then I'll report him.'

'Do you think he's a local person?'

'Sure to be.'

'Have you a reason for thinking that?'

'Mrs Selly knew him, I'm convinced of that. And he knew his way around Wolmering, too.'

She spoke with confidence. A formidable lady!

26

Perhaps the murderer wouldn't have found her a push-over, either. Standing there so squarely with her alert stick and determined, watchful grey eyes. She was in her sixties, had a broad, weathered face and short silver hair, tightly waved. She was the widow of a Trinity House official. She lived alone in a cottage a few doors from Vivienne's.

'Why do you think it was easy with Mrs Selly?'

'To start with, she was only a slip of a thing. Then she probably didn't know what he was up to until it was too late. The paper said she didn't struggle.'

'Wouldn't her dog have protected her?'

'I didn't see the dog.'

'I'd like to go over exactly what you did see.'

'Of course. I've done it before with Inspector Eyke, but there may still be some small thing I've overlooked.'

I scored more points to Mrs Lake. One didn't often receive such intelligent co-operation. I walked back with her to the far end of the green, beyond the look-out and the flag-pole. Now, turning about, one looked past the row of cannons to the foot-way where it ascended to the green, and immediately ahead to the last of the terrace villas and the slope leftward to the Town Green.

'I'd come from the Common, my usual walk, but I was going back the town way to post a letter. That's why I wasn't on the path. I was cutting across to Town Green.'

'Just a moment. Where did you go on the Common?'

'Nowhere near where you found her. I skirted along quite close to the houses. There's a fine view, looking down the coast.'

'Did you meet anybody?'

'Two people sitting on a bench, but too far off for me to recognise them. A girl riding a pony, ditto. Some people, strangers, fetching a car from the park.'

'Do you know George Selly by sight?'

'Yes.' She turned to me. 'Why haven't you questioned him?'

'We will,' I said. 'Carry on. Try to remember if you saw anyone else on the way here.'

'Well, I left the Common by the stile, and a car passed me, coming from the harbour. Then round the bend, looking towards the harbour, I saw a man walking in that direction.'

'Did you recognise him?'

'No. But there's the caravan site down there.'

'You can't describe him.'

'He was too far off. I think he was dressed just in shirt and trousers.'

'And he was the last person you saw?'

'Yes. Then I turned up here to the Guns. I leant on the rails there and smoked a gasper, trying to see the packet-boat that comes out of Harwich. If the horizon is clear you can just see her superstructure going along out there. She looks huge. But Tuesday was hazy. There was only a France, Fenwick boat, heading north.'

'Nobody passed while you watched the ships.'

'No.'

'Up here – or on the beach.'

She didn't reply at once, then she said: 'I think there was someone right down near the jetty.'

'That's the harbour way again.'

'Yes. It could have been caravanners, anyone. But nobody passed me up here, and the beach was the way you see it now.'

'Right. So you finished your cigarette.'

'Come along. We'll go over the same ground.'

I went with her across the green: not in a diagonal, but straying over to the brambles and the garden walls. Mrs Lake had a light, youthful step and seemed in little need of the stick. We reached a gate in one of the walls. It was just at the Town Green corner. Mrs Lake took two more steps, glanced across at the footway, and halted.

'Here.'

It was roughly seventy-five yards from where the footway dipped to the boat haul-up. There the path seemed to vanish into a cleft beyond which appeared nothing but grey sea.

'You'd be on the point of turning towards the town.'

'True, but not before I'd caught sight of her.'

'Would you swear to the identification?'

'Yes, I'd swear. If you remember I was able to describe her dress.'

'You waved to her, did you? One of your neighbours?'

Mrs Lake regarded me for a moment. 'I think you know the answer to that. I had no acquaintance with her. Mrs Selly could have had few friends in this town.'

'Not a passing word.'

'None.'

'But you looked across. Your eyes met.'

29

'I looked across from curiosity, to see who it was. Then as soon as I recognised her I looked away.'

'Yet you took in the dress with that one look.'

'Let's say it was the dress that helped me to recognise her. I'd seen her wearing it several times before, so as soon as I saw that I guessed who she was. But then of course I looked at her face and our eyes did meet very briefly. There was no mistake. I think she tossed her head: it was her usual reaction when she met me.'

'In addition you noticed she had no dog with her.'

'I have tried my best to be frank about that. I didn't notice it. But if it was off the lead, it could have been following her and I wouldn't have seen it.'

'You didn't see a dog up here at all?'

'No. And I am familiar with Mrs Selly's. It's an all-white wire-haired fox-terrier, a bitch. It has a limp in the right hind-leg.'

I nodded. 'So then you turned towards the town.'

'I posted my letter and went home.'

'You can add nothing to that.'

'I'm afraid I can't. It really is everything I remember.'

I thanked her: she was an excellent witness. But I suggested she should drop her project of watching for the murderer. She frowned and made some obscure motions with her stick.

'But you see . . . in a way . . . I feel responsible.'

And that was it: our last certain knowledge of the movements of Vivienne Selly. When I left the Guns I would have nothing to follow but my nose and dead reckoning. Her body had been found over a mile away, but almost certainly had been taken there by the murderer: a few faint signs of car tracks were visible in rough grass near the holm oaks. Where had she died? There was no clue, unless something could be read into the fact of her nakedness. Between the Guns and the holm oaks stretched a blank which so far we had been unable to fill.

Mrs Lake went her way. I decided I dare assume that Vivienne had continued her walk along the footway. After passing the look-out it turned inland and descended to join the road from the town to the harbour. Here stood a bench which commanded a view of the road, the river, the marshes, the caravan site: the latter having been relegated to a distance from the town which placed it out of earshot, if not out of sight. And here Vivienne had the choice of two directions: to the town (and the Common), or to the harbour. The first made an obvious round for an evening stroll: the latter extended the distance, and perhaps suggested an object.

I paused by the bench and tried to balance probabilities. She had been found on the Common, but that need have no significance. On the other hand we knew of no connection with the harbour or the caravans, and Eyke's ferreting there had provided no enlightenment. The one way she may have met some people (probably strangers) at the car park, a girl riding a pony, two people on a bench; the other, a strolling man who wasn't wearing a jacket and a person unspecified on the beach near the jetty. Likelihoods here? The car park was suggestive. It occupied a roadside strip beside the Common. Here Vivienne's murderer may have made contact and persuaded her (and the dog?) to get in his car. But the murder could not have taken place in a car (please accept this for the moment), and if he had driven Vivienne elsewhere, why return with the body? There were heaths and woods enough in the district to make such a risky proceeding unnecessary (one had to drive through the town to get access to the Common, and there was only a single road into the town). Thus it seemed to follow the murder occurred in the town, from which the Common would be the readiest place to dump a body; and this made the car park a less interesting proposition – contact might as well have been established where I was standing.

But still on this line (where the body was disposed): didn't it slightly favour the harbour? There was in fact a return road from the upper harbour which crossed the Common to the town. That road, a narrow one, was not much used, and it passed within half a mile of the holm oaks: was actually the road chosen by Eyke when he had driven me on to the Common. Against this, what need to dump the body on the Common if the crime had taken place in the harbour area? It could more easily have been slipped in the river, where the current would have taken it straight out to sea . . .

Logic at an impasse! When that happens, you turn your back and sniff the wind. I grunted to mark this stage in the proceedings and began to walk towards the harbour.

About a quarter of a mile. The road was level, with dunes on one side and marsh on the other. Passing at first a ribbon of drab chalets that ended at a café (closed). The sun had gone and we were in the long twilight. Some slants of smoke-mist hung over the ditches. Across the river I could see a huddle of buildings, one a shambling old timber place, painted white. Then, on my left, the stout skeleton of the jetty thrusting out towards the sea, and on my right, preluded by a toilet, the pastel-coloured ranks of the caravans.

Even here there seemed nobody about. That curious reticence extended everywhere. A few of the vans had lighted windows, but the others might easily have been empty. There was a light, too, in the harbourmaster's office, a small brick hut near the jetty; and over the river, in the timber building, where I could vaguely see someone working at a drawing-board. I walked to the quayside, which was lined with iron stanchions. Below me the water was running out fast. A small rusty coaster, equipped with dredging gear, creaked softly at moorings in an angle made by the jetty. A short distance upstream lay a raffle of wooden piers with a row of squat, tarred sheds behind them; above reared the spars and rigging of long-shore boats, while across the river were moored three yachts.

I glanced towards the jetty. Human interest at last! A man was lounging on the rails, smoking a pipe. He was dressed in jeans and a fisherman's navy jersey, and staring at me as I was staring at him. Had he lounged there on Tuesday . . . ? He perhaps belonged to the little coaster, though the vessel had a deserted, locked-up air; but however he seemed my only prospect, so I began walking towards the jetty. Then I stopped: I'd seen something else. An animal was loping across from the sand dunes. An off-white, halting, smudge of an animal: a wire-haired fox-terrier. With a limp.

I knew at once it was the right dog, even before the limp registered. I'd felt that sudden click one experiences when instinct jumps ahead of reason. The dog was tousled, rough-looking, had clearly been living out of doors; was trailing a bit of broken lead on which it now and then stumbled. It was trundling along self-intently, as though quite content to be its own master. Then it saw me and pulled up short: stood deciding if I were friend or enemy.

I made conciliatory noises. I am no dog-man, though I can usually get along with animals (I have been long convinced that even fish have unsuspected intelligence and personality). I could feel this animal's suspicion, its quick impulse to stay aloof from me; I tried to conquer it by smiling, stooping low, making friendly sounds. No go. The dog growled a soft warning. It was not minded to make my acquaintance. Having established this point it backed off once or twice, then turned and loped away from me, towards the jetty.

The jetty was a cul-de-sac. I followed up eagerly, working to the left to cover the sand dunes. The smoker on the jetty seemed to fathom my intentions since he put away his pipe and took some steps from the rails. At first the dog didn't seem to notice him. It padded on to the jetty with complete unconcern. Then the man spread his arms and began covering movements and the dog yelped and skittered on the sandy concrete. I moved up quickly. Now the dog realised that we had it in a trap. It cowered between us, showing its teeth, growling, dripping saliva.

'Watch him,' the man said. 'I think he'll bite.'

I felt a moment of surprise when I heard his voice. But the dog had begun feinting from one to the other of us, snarling angrily and snapping its teeth.

'Go for his collar!'

The dog made its decision. It came my way, on the side opposite to the rails. There it was a ten-foot drop into the water and I daren't lunge confidently in that direction. The dog judged things nicely, but as it scuttled by it tripped on the tag-end of the lead: yelped, came down on its shoulder, and disappeared over the side.

'Hell – that's it!' the man exclaimed.

We hastened to the edge and stared down. The dog had surfaced, but the swirling ebb was carrying it seawards at a good six knots. Beyond the mouth of the river stretched a broad fan where the fresh water mingled with the salt, and through it the current hurried unchecked as far as eye could trace its movement.

'The poor bastard!' the man jerked at me. 'That's the dog you've been looking for, isn't it?'

'Is there a boat—?'

'It's no use. He'll be gone before you can get to him.'

He added something, I couldn't hear what: it sounded like 'Might as well!' – and the next moment, before I could lay a hand on him, he'd jumped off the jetty after the dog.

Sheer madness!

I raced along the jetty bawling: 'You bloody fool – come back!' But if he heard me he paid no attention, and there was very little prospect of him coming back. The current was rushing him out to sea as fast as I could keep pace on the jetty, and he was assisting it with long, confident strokes in the direction of the dog. I reached the end of the jetty. A lifebuoy hung there. I grabbed it, shouted, pitched it in ahead of him. He brushed it aside with an irritable gesture and continued to launch himself towards Holland.

'You fool. You bloody fool!'

I was chattering with anger, shock and helplessness. But if the fool was to be snatched from his folly it couldn't be done from the end of the jetty. I bolted back again. The harbour-master's office was only a dozen yards from the jetty. I threw open the door and burst in panting, to find an elderly man writing at a desk.

'A man has just jumped off the jetty!'

The harbour-master (I assumed) stared at me over half-glasses. Then he picked up the phone beside him, said: 'Get me Fred, will you?' – and tucked the instrument under his chin.

'Who was the man?'

'How should I know!'

'Could he swim?'

'Yes, yes!'

'Right. Then get you back there, old partner, and keep your eye on him, or he's a gonner.'

The patois sank in; I rushed from the office and pounded up the jetty again. Keep an eye on him! But already he'd have vanished in the thickening gloom of the twilight. At first I saw nothing but grey wrinkled water fining and blurring into the horizon, and it was only after staring till the tears came that I caught a glimpse of a speck of white. The lifebuoy: he'd be near that: they were both being carried by the same current! At least now I had his rough direction and could point it out to possible rescuers. I scoured round the jetty for a splinter of driftwood and laid it out on the bearing of the lifebuoy. Then I jogged up and down impatiently, willing the rescue boat to arrive.

About then it struck me: was it just possible that I'd been making a fool of myself? After all, I knew nothing about the fellow in the blue jersey, and certainly there'd been no panic in *his* demeanour. He had set off with confident, unhurried strokes, like a man who knew how to pace himself over a distance; and I couldn't help recalling that touch of irritability when I'd dropped the lifebuoy in his path. Then there was the accent – not that of a fisherman; it suggested intelligence, cultivation. And the quick impression I'd received of his face was of well-modelled features and lively eyes. A man of about my age. Was he some well-heeled resident who liked to swan around in a fisherman's outfit – and an ex-Channel-swimmer on top, quite capable of throwing off a few sea miles?

But I wasn't left long to wonder. An engine buzzed waspishly up the harbour. Within seconds a rubber inshore rescue-boat came busily slamming down the tide. It spun to a brisk stop by the jetty and one of the two men grabbed an iron rung. The other, a burly fellow with a frieze of beard, throttled back the engine and squinted up at me.

'Can you give us a bearing?'

I checked with my piece of driftwood. 'Say ten degrees south of the line of the jetty. Watch for a lifebuoy. I threw one near him. I saw it two minutes ago on that bearing.'

'How far out?'

'Say half a mile.'

'When did he fall in?'

'Seven minutes ago.'

The bearded man thumbed the throttle and the boat surged away, to take up a course, it seemed to me, a good deal too far to the south.

And in the end, I have to admit, I was mildly pink about the ears. Just half-an-hour later they fetched my man into the harbour-master's office. He was sodden of course, but in no way distressed, and was clearly well-known to the harbour-master and the boat-crew. He gave the former a broad grin and me rather a sheepish one.

'Sorry. The poor devil sank before I got to him.'

'I should think he did,' said the harbour-master dryly. 'I reckoned this was one of your tricks, Mr Reymerston. I've laid out your size of gear in the store.'

The man, Reymerston, went into the store to change, and the harbour-master poured out some cocoa he'd been heating.

'So you know him,' I said.

'Oh, ah. Pretty well. There's not many people don't know Mr Reymerston.'

'He must be a good swimmer.'

'He's a funny man in the water. And there's people about who reckon he can paint.'

'He's an artist, then?'

The harbour-master looked sidelong. 'Depends a bit on what you call art. But I tell you straight, if I owned a fishing-boat I wouldn't pay Mr Reymerston to do its picture.'

When Reymerston came out I asked him questions about Tuesday, then left him to drink cocoa and chat with the others. I had already put my questions to them and added a few more negatives to the grand total. But the dog was crossed off. Now I knew it had been with Vivienne. For a moment, through the dog, I had almost touched her. And though the dog had gone now, like its mistress, it had left me with a clue.

The other half of its lead.

CHAPTER THREE

A STRANGE THOUGHT: fourteen hours earlier I
hadn't known that a Vivienne Selly existed.
Now she was as familiar to me as a sister who I was
meeting again after a long absence. I wasn't liking her
very much, but that was irrelevant: Vivienne was one
of the family; one of a big, sad family, none of whom
I'd met in the living flesh.

The way she'd died. This was unusual and somehow
oddly appropriate to Wolmering. A genteel death.
She'd been suffocated in a way that left no traces. I
didn't know how. There is usually bruising and other
superficial injury. The victim struggles, breaks her
nails, has to be wrestled with, struck. Not so in Vivienne's case. The body was curiously immaculate. Not
a scratch or a bruise, and the nails prettily manicured,
and clean, as though they had been lately scrubbed.
The face had set in a relaxed expression, simply blank
and dead, and the limbs lay naturally and straight,
with the fingers of each hand gently curled. She
hadn't been drugged and there had been no inter-
course. Her clothes had not been rumpled or torn.

It was as though, expecting death, she had calmly undressed, laid down, composed herself, and died. Rather uncanny. Yet, as I said, strangely appropriate to Wolmering.

George Selly. The reason we hadn't questioned him was, frankly, because we hadn't been able to lay our hands on him. George Selly was missing, though whether by accident or design was a question that remained open. He lived at Castleford, seventy miles off, with a widow, a Mrs Bacon; but when the local C.I.D. visited her house on Wednesday afternoon they found it locked and the garage empty. Selly was a rep for the Corstophine Drug Co. Ltd, an Edinburgh firm of manufacturing chemists. All they could tell us was that he had time-off due to him which he was free to take when it suited him. Mrs Bacon had stopped her tradesmen for the following ten days and had paid them up to date, but the couple had told nobody where they were going and as yet we had no lead at all. Selly a likely culprit? Difficult to judge without actually having observed the man. He was paying Vivienne a fair allowance *(vide* her bank), and she was keeping him out of a valuable little property. But against that he was earning a comfortable income as Corstophine's East Anglian rep, and with the new divorce law on the book he'd be free of her anyway in a year or so. Also the style of the crime seemed wrong. Between husband and wife one would have expected some violence. Then there was the circumstance of Selly coming from outside and the body being left at the far end of the heath. Nothing logically conclusive of course – that's a rarity in criminal investigation

– but enough to make me leave a question-mark beside Selly and to keep a keen eye on the field.

The style of the crime. What you had to rule out was robbery and sex, unless the latter was psychopathic to a degree I hadn't met with. Possible (one must consider everything) but only on the margin of probability: leaving the more familiar motives like hindrance, threat, blackmail. Hindrance was Selly's motive. Threat and blackmail remained. Of these, as yet, no indication, but we were in the early days of the case. Perhaps more important at the moment was that curious and gentle execution, an almost reverent, affectionate killing, done without any sign of hatred. Who would kill in such a way? A person of strong sensibilities. A merciful person, and intelligent enough to perform the deed in the way it was done. A lover? No, he would kill passionately. A relative? None in the picture, except Selly. A woman? This was worth hesitating over, because the picture did include women.

Friday morning: I breakfasted with Eyke in the coffee-room at the Pelican. The Pelican is the best hotel in town and Eyke booked me in there as a matter of course. I liked Eyke. He was one of those slow-spoken, conscientious provincial Inspectors, very careful, very responsible, never likely to be rushed into a wrong decision. Tallish, solidly built, brown-eyed, his cropped hair very grey for forty-five, he had a slightly heavy, fresh-complexioned face with a wry nose, got through boxing.

He brought news. Selly's car had been seen in

Carlisle. It had been misparked during yesterday's lunch-hour and a warden had written it a ticket. Unfortunately this news wasn't filtered to the police until late in the evening, by which time Selly was long gone, north or south as the case might be.

'I think he's in Scotland, sir,' Eyke ventured. 'If he's touring it fits about right. He couldn't have left Castleford very early yesterday because Mrs Bacon was there when the baker called at one p.m. So they probably left in the afternoon and spent the night on the road somewhere. Then yesterday they'd be at Carlisle for lunch. I'd say that Castleford only just missed them.'

'It all sounds very innocent.'

'Well, you don't know, sir. He may have rigged it to look like that. And he couldn't have known the body would be found straight away, so this trip to Scotland may have been a sort of alibi.'

'The story didn't make the papers on Wednesday?'

'No sir. And they didn't give it much of a spread yesterday.'

'So he could have missed seeing it.'

'Yes sir, he could've done. Murder isn't the eye-catcher it was in the old days.'

Eyke was deferential. Some of the police in the provinces are veiledly hostile to talent from the Yard. Not Eyke: he had a crime that was strange to him, and he was genuinely grateful to be given a specialist. We discussed the dog. It must, we decided, have been living rough around the town since Tuesday; if it had stayed on the Common or the marshes adjacent it could very well have passed unnoticed. There was nothing to be surmised from its appearance at the harbour, where a scavenging dog might naturally stray; but its being in the town made it now virtually a certainty that it was there the crime had been committed. Vivienne would not have been voluntarily separated from her dog: it must have accompanied her to wherever she'd been lured. There, either she or the murderer had tied it up, and subsequently it had broken its lead and escaped.

'You're assuming she went into a house, sir.'

'I think the manner of her death requires it. There was no struggle. She'd have been lying down somewhere. There had to be a very soft pillow handy.'

'Then like that it's someone who lives in the town.'

'That was the most likely prospect from the start.'

Eyke looked down his wry nose a little: it wasn't a prospect that appealed to him.

'It may have been a visitor, sir.'

'Perhaps. But the balance of facts is against it. If it had been a sex crime now, or a robbery. But what we've got points to a resident.'

Eyke sighed and nodded. 'So it comes down to this, sir. House-to-house enquiries.'

'I'm afraid it does. And watch out for the lead. It's the one thing we have that ties our man to the job.'

Eyke had only a sergeant and two D.C.s; I suggested we called in help from Eastwich. Eyke was up in arms directly, so I dropped the idea for the moment. We'd make a start, I told him, with the houses bordering the Common, and commencing in the area of the car park; also we'd follow up people who used the car park regularly and who'd left cars there Tuesday evening. Eyke was cheered by the latter instruction.

'Most of those will be visitors.'

I grinned. 'But don't neglect the houses.'

Eyke smiled shyly. We were going to make a good team.

My own car (the Lotus) was in dock, and M/T had supplied me with a Cortina. I drew it from the cramped yard of the Pelican and tinkered it slowly down Wolmering's High Street. A modest street. Its most ambitious building was the Pelican itself, a tall, elegantly veranda'd example of the Georgian, partly festooned with a tree-like creeper. The front was recessed at one side to permit a bow that ran up to the eaves, with semicircular extensions of the verandas; giving it a ramparted appearance. It fronted a triangle at the top of the street which probably once had been a green but which now, paved and ornamented with a town sign, offered a little free parking and a site for half-a-dozen stalls. For the rest the High Street was a mixture of undistinguished period and dull Victorian buildings: almost drab, yet somehow expressing the relaxed, loitering flavour of Wolmering. No traffic warden, and Eyke had boasted you could leave your car unlocked for days.

I drifted on: you couldn't hurry; pedestrians tended to share the street with you. Many were elderly, well-dressed people of whom Mrs Lake was the type. The High Street was their boulevard where they shopped, gossiped and drank coffee; or introduced coltish grand-children from this or that university. The shops were largely their shops. I noticed two displaying fashionable clothes; a good florist, a well-stocked bookshop,

45

a cake-shop advertising brick-oven baking. A well-bred town. I didn't think the gossip was over-much engaged with Vivienne Selly. In life and death she didn't belong here, and God willing, her murderer didn't either.

At its lower end the High Street split and passed to each side of a craft-shop. It was about here that one became aware of an invisible line running through the town. Not blatantly a class-line: nothing so crude, it could be legitimately described in terms of architecture. To the south of the line the style was prevailingly Georgian, to the north Victorian, with an outer skin of modern. Yet in effect it did serve as a class-line; you could tell that without meeting the inhabitants. The commodious, though dreary, 1880 terrace houses were a step below the cramped but highly-decorated ex-fishermen's cottages. The unfortunate pier was below the line, and so were the sea-front hotel and boarding-houses. The great ornamented flint church, with its inevitable green, made the line take a respectful bend round its precincts. Class: very subtle, but distinct; and the Sellys, perhaps in ignorance, had stepped over the line. To the north, among the tweenwar suburban semis, they might have put down comfortable roots in the hierarchy.

I passed the craft-shop and coasted down a gradient through the low-caste terraces. These ended in a garage and a glimpse of thirties modern, after which one crossed a bridge over a creek that bounded the town. Coming and going you crossed the bridge: there was no other access to Wolmering. If Vivienne

46

had not been murdered in the town she had crossed that bridge twice, once alive, once dead. I glanced back at it in the mirror. No, my reasoning was sound: she had died in town. There was no purpose to be served by returning with the body when there were remote spots everywhere to hand.

Another gradient took me away from the bridge and through a strip of extra-mural development; then I was clear of the town and following the line of a low bluff, with the Wolmer and its marshes below on my left. Just ahead, also left, was strung a line of closely-clipped yews, above which I could see a screen of copper beeches and the roofs and dormers of a large house. Huntingfield School. About a mile out of town. I slowed before a pair of open wrought-iron gates. On the gravel before the house were parked ten or twelve cars, including Pamela Rede's red Mini. I parked beside them.

A faint smell of apples and a sensation of warmth, like the warmth of a beehive (or a jail). From behind a door, a carefully modulated voice, flattened by the acoustics of an occupied class-room. A middle-aged woman in an overall was polishing the black-and-white tiles with a cloth placed over a mop: she paused to look up suspiciously as she heard my step on the metal grille.

'Yes – what is it?'

At the moment, her eyes said, she was the guardian of this institution.

'Detective Chief Superintendent Gently. I'd like a word with Miss Swefling.'

'Is it an appointment?'

'No.'

'Well, I'm afraid Miss Swefling is busy.'

But her eyes switched briefly to the broad staircase that rose from the hall to a railed landing.

I smiled at her and went up. She stood staring hostilely, but didn't intervene. The staircase, which had shallow marble steps, made a handsome turn through a half-circle. The landing was spacious enough to be called a mezzanine and had a polished floor and a carpet. It was furnished with low book-cases containing children's classics, and above these were taped some youthful watercolours. Several doors led off. One was glass-panelled; I could see through it girls sitting at their desks; and though I made no sound on the soft carpet, every head was turned in my direction. A voice snapped imperatively: the heads jerked round, but then one or two covertly looked again; bright-eyed, giggling little girls of about eight or nine, in cream blouses and plum skirts. I moved out of their vision. At the far end of the mezzanine was a panelled oak door inscribed: Knock – and Wait. I knocked twice. A firm voice said: 'Enter', and I opened the door and went in.

A woman was seated at a big pedestal desk with a graph-paper chart spread before her. She was shading-in squares with red and black pens and didn't immediately take notice of my entry. The room was large and lofty and sunny. The walls were lined with glass-fronted varnished bookcases. Other than these there were two filing-cabinets and three pleasant mahogany chairs with red plush seats. On the walls hung several watercolour landscapes by a nineteenth-century painter who I couldn't identify, and on the floor was a fine Persian carpet with colours too delicate for it not to have been expensive. I closed the door. The woman finished her shading and laid her pens on a tray. Then she looked up. Her eyes went large, her expression quite blank.

'Miss Swefling?'

'I am Miss Swefling.'

'I'm Chief Superintendent Gently.'

'Yes. Your picture was in *The East Anglian Daily Times*. But I'm not sure you are welcome here, Superintendent.'

'I'm sorry. Why is that?'

'Because our reputation has suffered quite enough. I would consider it a kindness if you kept away from Huntingfield and had no further contact with our girls.'

One of the chairs was placed in front of the desk, perhaps for the reception of erring pupils. I came forward and sat myself on it. Miss Swefling watched me with cold eyes. She was in her late forties; an attractive woman. She had an oval face with a widish jaw. Her hair, barely touched with grey streaks, was luxuriant and worn medium-long. She'd be on the tall side, and as far as I could see had a full and handsome figure. She had strong but pretty hands. She was wearing a grey dress with blue facings.

'Perhaps you'll be good enough to state your business.'

'Certainly. I'm investigating the death of Mrs Selly.'

'But the four girls who were acquainted with her have already been questioned.'

'For that reason I find it necessary to extend my enquiries.'

'I'm not sure I understand you.'

'It's very straightforward. I'm trying to reconstruct the events of Tuesday. The four girls left Mrs Selly at about four p.m. I want to know who saw her after that.'

Miss Swefling looked away. 'I still don't understand you. There were no late passes issued on Tuesday. If you are referring to our day-girls, my suggestion is you approach them through their parents.'

She wasn't going to be helpful. I didn't mind. She had already given me a positive reaction. There was something to dig for, I was sure of it; from the moment she turned away her eyes. I waited. Her eyes came back to me. They were greenish and stern, under strong brows.

'Of course I appreciate your position, Miss Swefling. I am told your school has a high reputation. It is unfortunate that pupils of Huntingfield should have come under the influence of such a person as Mrs Selly. Naturally, you would need to take prompt and effective action when the facts came to your notice.'

'I could scarcely do less than that.'

'You would insist on an end to the association.'

She said nothing.

'With absolute firmness. For example, you might have to threaten the culprits with expulsion.'

'Well?'

'Isn't that what happened?'

Miss Swefling's hands moved, then were still. 'Whatever action I took is an internal matter. I am not obliged to discuss it with the police.'

'But you did take some action?'

'Perhaps I did.'

'In fact the association had come to your notice?'

A hand flickered. 'I would be a poor headmistress if such things went on outside my knowledge.'

'Then you knew.'

'Very well – I knew.'

'Would you care to enlarge on that, Miss Swefling?'

She hesitated briefly, staring a little past me; then she said firmly, 'No.'

I gestured. 'You'll understand my curiosity. I'm sure you are a very perceptive headmistress. But this association had been going on for around twelve months before, apparently, you became aware of it. And that happened at a strangely critical moment. Within a few hours Mrs Selly was dead. You are too intelligent not to appreciate the importance of my knowing how you came by your information.'

'That was . . . coincidental.'

'I daren't take your word for it.'

'I'm afraid you must.'

I shook my head. 'Either you tell me or I will have to assume it is significant. In which case I must make very extensive enquiries.'

Miss Swefling coloured. 'That sounds like blackmail.'

'I am simply advising you of the alternative. I don't want to waste valuable time, but I must have an answer to my question.'

I settled myself on the plush-seated chair, as though to prepare for a lengthy session. Miss Swefling stared silently for some moments, her eyes angry, longing to attack. A bell sounded mutedly; it was followed by a murmuring, a slamming of desk-lids, shuffling of feet. Miss Swefling's eyes darted away, came back to me. She let them fall to the chart on the desk.

'Very well. I received an anonymous letter.'

'I will see it if I may.'

'I'm afraid you can't. I destroyed it.'

I ghosted a shrug and said nothing.

'You believe me, don't you?'

'A pity you don't have the letter.'

'But, good heavens! I'm telling you the truth. I received it by the second post on Tuesday, here, at this desk. I don't tell lies.'

'A hand-written letter?'

'No, it was typed: very neatly done on good paper. It mentioned the four girls by name and warned me they had a scandalous relation with Mrs Selly.'

'Posted in Wolmering?'

'Yes.'

'The address was correct?'

'Yes. And if you wish to know, in my opinion the writer was an educated person.'

I said quickly: 'Then who was it?'

She stared, her eyes growing large. 'I have told you already that the letter was anonymous. Whether you accept it or not, that is the truth.'

'But you can guess.'

'No.'

'It shouldn't be difficult, Miss Swefling.'

She set her lips firmly together and determinedly stared at the chart.

'I'll do the guessing then.'

She said nothing.

'Three of the four girls involved are boarders.'

'That means nothing!'

'Quite the opposite. I think we both feel it means a lot. The letter was posted in Wolmering. We must assume it came from someone concerned about the girls. The parents of three of them live at a distance, which leaves only the guardians of Miss Rede. Wasn't that your conclusion?'

'It is too absurd! Major Rede wouldn't write an anonymous letter.'

'Nor Mrs Rede?'

'Nor she either. Quite obviously you haven't met these people.'

'They are too forthright.'

'Exactly. They would have told me straight out.'

'Unless there was some reason why they should not?'

Miss Swefling gave a scornful snatch of her head.

I didn't persist, but I made a mental note to query Major Rede with Eyke. If a normally outspoken person had written an anonymous letter it might be worthwhile enquiring why. Of course it could just as well be coincidental and merely juxtaposed to the crime: some crimes seem to attract the coincidental. Routine was invented to grapple with the irrelevant.

'Leaving that. You received the letter. Apparently you didn't question the contents.'

'I may have questioned them, but I couldn't ignore them. Nobody in my position would do that.'

'You felt the information was probable.'

Miss Swefling flushed sharply. 'That is an unfair insinuation. Probable or not, it was possible, and it was my duty to take notice.' She grabbed a pen and began to flex it. 'Naturally, the girls here are like all girls. However strict the supervision it is impossible entirely to contain emotional adjustments. It may even be undesirable. There are schools of thought of that opinion. Here, we acknowledge that emotional stresses exist, but we try to keep them at low temperature.'

'But you do have failures.'

'We have our percentage.'

'Recent ones?'

The pen bent in a bow. 'Since it is a matter of record I can scarcely deny it. Yes. A teacher left us in the Easter term.'

I nodded. 'So then this affair with Mrs Selly was a serious matter. Coming on the heels of a similar business, it had to be dealt with energetically.'

'I took the steps I thought proper.'

'You would give the girls an ultimatum.'

'I spoke to them that same afternoon. I forbade them further acquaintance with Mrs Selly.'

'But would that have been enough?'

'Under pain of expulsion. It is an extremely effective deterrent.'

'To girls who leave at the end of the term anyway?'

Miss Swefling bent the pen, saying nothing.

'I think,' I said, 'you'd have taken a stronger line, bearing in mind the earlier scandal. Your reputation, the school's reputation, couldn't stand a repetition of that. So what would you do? You couldn't stop short at merely disciplining the girls. Mrs Selly was the root of the trouble. You'd have to see Mrs Selly.'

The pen snapped. Miss Swefling sat staring at the two ragged ends.

'Did you see her?'

Her mouth curled bitterly. 'Isn't that why you are here now?'

'I am investigating her death.'

'I had nothing to do with that.'

'But you can help me.'

'That's a familiar phrase.'

She laid down the broken pen, rose and went over to the large window. I was right about her figure. I wondered why she hadn't married. Through the window one looked over a gravelled quadrangle and past the beeches to some tennis courts: then, beyond rhododendrons, to the western end of the Common. Miss Swefling stood staring in that direction. About half a mile away would be the grove of holm oaks.

'I suppose you know I was in the town Tuesday evening.'

I didn't: it had occurred to nobody to check Miss Swefling's movements.

'I was lecturing the Literary and Scientific Society. I am giving them a course on The French Novel.'

'At what time was that?'

'At seven forty-five. At the Agnes Strickland Hall in Camp Road. The lecture lasts about an hour, then there's a period for questions. After that I sometimes drive back, sometimes have supper with some of the officials. Tuesday evening I stayed on.' She hesitated. 'The chairman this year is Mrs Rede.'

'You had supper at her house?'

'No. We were invited by the treasurer, Captain Scott-Wemys.'

'When did you leave there?'

'It would be nearly eleven. But that has nothing to do with the matter. What interests you is when I arrived, which would be a little after seven.' She leaned forward, pressing against the sill. 'That was when I visited Mrs Selly.'

I said nothing. She remained at the window, pushing at the sill with little rhythmic pressures: somehow girlish, appealing. From behind, she didn't look more than thirty. In a flash I guessed she would be popular with the girls: had perhaps experienced 'emotional stresses' herself. But I didn't doubt she had resisted them with all the considerable steel in her nature.

'Frankly, I don't think I can help you.'

'How did Mrs Selly receive you?'

'How would you expect?'

'As I have come to know her, I think she may have wept on your shoulder.'

Miss Swefling turned, her eyes wide. 'My goodness. My goodness.'

'Well?'

'You're entirely right. And after that she tried to seduce me.'

She came back to the desk and sat, facing me with still-surprised eyes. I hunched a shoulder.

'Vivienne was lonely.'

'Yes. She appalled me, but that's about the truth.'

'She'd had the girls. You were taking them away from her. She hadn't the spirit left to blackguard you.'

'I know, I know. She was wretchedly miserable.'

'When you turned her down, she was on her own.'

Miss Swefling gave a little quivering shudder. 'It was ghastly. It made me feel ill. I was expecting her to be brazen and abusive. That sort of thing I know how to handle. But she just listened sullenly. Then she fell apart. I had her kneeling and weeping in my lap. Then she started kissing me and trying to make love. I grabbed my bag and got out of there quickly.'

'And you left her – how?'

'She was snivelling on the floor.'

'In a very depressed state.'

'I suppose that's true. But good heavens, what else could I have done?'

I shrugged. 'Not much. It was beginning to be too late.'

Miss Swefling went still, her eyes locking with mine. 'You're not suggesting this is connected with what happened later?'

'I think it might be. She was very depressed. She may have felt compelled to try some desperate course.'

'But that's . . . horrifying.'

'There are facts to explain.'

'It means that I am partly to blame.'

I shook my head. 'You'd be just a factor in the case. Perhaps it was going to happen anyway, sooner or later.'

She hesitated, eyes widening. 'And you – you're quite cold-blooded about all this! It's just a mechanism you're trying to understand, people, their feelings: bits of a machine.'

'Is there any other way to do my job?'

'It's terrible: sickening. A despicable business.'

'Perhaps a moral surgery.'

'It's the negation of all pity!'

I grunted. 'Pity is a private thing.'

She snatched her eyes away from mine and sat glowering at one of the handsome watercolours. Well, I'd seen this happen before. In the long annals of my sad family plenty of people had called me inhuman. But the surgeon in the theatre must not be as other men. That privilege waits till he peels off his gloves. Someone had laid Vivienne on my table, and the tool I had to use wasn't pity.

'I have one or two more questions.'

She gave me a bitter, quelling look. 'I was almost forgetting you were a policeman. Just now. But you were only being clever, weren't you?'

'How long were you with Mrs Selly?'

'Twenty minutes.' She jerked the answer contemptuously.

'How was she dressed?'

'In nothing and a dressing-gown. And a drenching of cheap scent.'

'Was she alone?'

'That was my assumption.'

'You noticed nothing to the contrary?'

'No. And she would scarcely have behaved in the way she did if there had been an audience.'

'Did you threaten her?'

'Perhaps I gave that impression.'

'Did she threaten you?'

'Is that likely?'

'Quite likely, Miss Swefling. You were alone with her. An unscrupulous woman could turn that to her advantage.'

'Well, she didn't.'

'She said nothing like this: "You can't touch me because the girls are eighteen. But I can swear you came here for a certain purpose, and I can get the girls to back me up." '

Miss Swefling blushed furiously. 'That's vile!'

'But not an uncommon line of defence.'

'It is ugly, vicious. I won't listen any longer. I've told you everything you've a right to expect.'

'One thing more. Where was your car parked?'

'I don't remember!' She was rising to her feet.

'I'd like you to remember. It will save us checking.'

'Oh my God! Beside the Common!'

I went. She swept open the door for me so that she could close it after me with a slam. Unfortunate. In other circumstances I would have been happy to make a friend of Miss Swefling. Her face had a stern-ness that was close to sympathy and her eyes were expressive without calculation. But there was that undercurrent of impetuosity, and certainly she had strong hands. In the hall I picked up a prospectus which told me her Christian name was Marianne. She had been educated at Girton but had not, it appeared, taken her doctorate.

CHAPTER FOUR

A ND SO, PURSUING my inhuman way, I was beginning to get a picture that focused: when Vivienne
Selly set out from her cottage she was deeply depressed
and perhaps feeling she had little to lose. Alien in her
environment, abandoned by her husband, stripped of
her emotional contacts, humiliated and rejected: if
she had thrown herself off the jetty it would not have
been a surprising conclusion. But this she hadn't done:
so what did she do? What had been Vivienne's last
throw? My only clue lay in the fact that she had taken
pains to dress herself neatly. She might have thrown
on any old clothes (like the slacks and sweater that lay
dumped on a chair) – but no: after Miss Swefling left,
she had decked herself out in a modish dress. She must
have done this directly. There had been only half-
an-hour for it between Miss Swefling's leaving and
her own setting-out. Whatever her intention, it had
been in her mind from the moment the door closed
on Miss Swefling. So it was perhaps a course of action
which she had meditated previously but had regarded
as too risky, but which now, in her desperation, she

was prepared to implement straight away. No sudden brainstorm: what she was about had its roots in the past.

But for whom would she have dressed up? In Vivienne's case the matter was doubtful. She was ambisexual, and the manner of the crime offered no indication of the gender of the criminal. On balance one might assume it was a man because the body had been handled and transported, but against that Vivienne had weighed only eight stone and so was not beyond manipulation by a woman. In addition, on current form, Vivienne's preference seemed to lie with the ladies, so these considerations cancelled out: the question of gender stayed open. But man or woman, this much was certain: they represented some answer to Vivienne's distress; while just as certainly, she had represented a threat which they had been unable to ignore. So, briefly, we were looking for a person with something to hide; who had been acquainted previously with Vivienne; who she thought was capable of solving her problems; and who probably lived within walking distance of her cottage. A narrowed field: but balanced, alas, on grounds of logical probability. Vivienne might equally well have dressed prettily to cheer herself up; and by so doing have attracted a casual predator.

On the routine side, there would be no harm in checking Miss Swefling's account of her movements. The estimated time of death covered a span from nine p.m. to midnight. Vivienne might have sought a second interview. Her walk might have taken her to the Agnes Strickland Hall. Failing contact there, she might have followed Miss Swefling to Captain Scott-Wemys' house, and then to her car: significantly, parked beside the Common. And there was another angle about the Common – it bounded the grounds of Huntingfield School. It was probably open to Miss Swefling to drive on the Common without first having to drive through the town. The way had been clear for her to take Vivienne back with her, perhaps pretending to consent to Vivienne's advances; then, having smothered Vivienne as she lay in bed, to transport the body to the grove of holm oaks. Between eleven and midnight there were unlikely to be watchers, and Miss Swefling's rooms could be remote from the dormitories in any case.

Other prospects? Pamela Rede's guardian had been revealed on the edge of the scene. He wasn't confirmed as the writer of that anonymous letter, but I remembered the look Diane Culpho had given Pamela. Did Diane guess the letter came from that quarter? Possible even that she suspected Pamela? Just thinking aloud, Pamela didn't have an alibi that one could check with any certainty. The same might conceivably apply to her guardian, whose wife was attending Miss Swefling's lecture; interesting point. But until I'd met the gentleman there was no profit in further surmise. What we were short of, and what I most needed, were names of people known to have associated with Vivienne. She was too lonely. In the background, somewhere, were acquaintances routine hadn't given us; yet.

Outside the police-station: a blue 3.8 Jaguar of recent date-letter, handsomely polished. Inside: George

Alexander Selly, Corstophine Drug Co. Ltd's East Anglian representative.

I didn't like Selly. We shared the same Christian name, which always gives rise to a slight hostility. Also I'd had the feeling that he was outside the case, and that his choosing to disappear had made gratuitous work for us. But these were pinpricks, like the Jaguar (redundant power + weight = dinosaur); it was when I walked into Eyke's office and set eyes on him that I knew I didn't like George Selly.

He was a tall, bulky man. Though the day was warm he was wearing a short astrakhan coat over a well-cut lounge suit, and beneath the suit an embroidered waistcoat with small gilt buttons, shaped like horse-shoes. He had a plump, grey-jowled face, with aggressive eyes under emphatic brows; a dominating nose, tooth-brush moustache, and sleekly oiled-and-combed hair. It was a face that carried a threat: accept what I say to you or else: and went with a hard, loud voice quick with scorn and self-justification. A bully: a commando of the hard sell. No doubt there was a background of insecurity. But I couldn't persuade myself to view him clinically; he made disliking him a positive pleasure.

He had just arrived, and already he was trying to put Eyke in his place. Eyke introduced us. Selly shot out a hand which I left hanging in the air. I took my seat at Eyke's desk. Selly sat down angrily across from me. Eyke took a notepad and pencil from the desk and sat on a chair to my right. I looked at Selly. I said smoothly:

'I suppose you know we've been looking for you, Mr Selly?'

'Looking for me!' His eyes slammed at me. 'Then you didn't look very far, did you?'

'Where have you been?'

'Where? On my lawful occasions, that's where.'

'I shall need details.'

'You can bloody have them. I've got them right here in my pocket.'

He pulled out a fat pig-skin wallet from which peeped a wad of fivers. He separated two folded papers and threw them on the desk. They were hotel bills.

'There. You can't get over those, can you? One for The Crown, Harrogate, Wednesday night. One for The Lion, Sleaford, yesterday.'

'You stayed at these places?'

'That's what I'm telling you.'

'They seem an unusual combination.'

He rolled his eyes. 'It was an unusual trip, wasn't it? I'm supposed to be booking in at Oban tonight.' He returned the wallet to his pocket. 'Look, there's no need to come the high horse with me. I broke my trip just as soon as I knew, whether I could be any help or not. I'd got ten days, you know that? I might have effed off and left you to it. I haven't seen Viv for going on a twelve-month. I reckon I'm the injured party round here.'

'You are not concerned by your wife's death?'

'All right, I am! It shouldn't have happened. But you know, I know, we'd parted company, so what's the point in pulling a long face?'

'I still want your movements in more detail.'

'Right. Beginning on lunchtime Wednesday. We set out from Castleford at two and got into Harrogate at twenty-past six.'

'We?'

He sneered. 'It's jam for you. I'm living with a widow, Cathy Bacon. I dropped her off at the Pelican, but she's around if you need confirmation. So that's that. And yesterday morning I phoned a booking to the Ancaster Arms, Callander, but we only got as far as Carlisle when I bought a paper with the news in it. So I'm shocked. I was through with Viv, but she didn't deserve that. She was just a pathetic bitch who didn't know how to cope with life. Well, I turned the Jag round and we finished up at Sleaford last night. Then this morning I drove here. Now you know all about it.'

'Why didn't you report to the Carlisle police?'

Selly snickered. 'Some hope of that! The way it was put in the *Telegraph* they'd have brought me down here in handcuffs.'

'It would also have saved us some trouble.'

'Trouble you are paid to live with, mate. Which is more than I am, coming back here. I can't write this lot off as expenses.'

'That sometimes happens at the death of relatives.'

Selly gave me a queer look. 'Well anyway, I came, for what it's worth. You know now I haven't gone into hiding.' He rose. 'Will that be all?'

I shook my head. 'I'm only just beginning.'

'How do you mean?'

'I want your movements on Tuesday.'

Selly's eyes slammed at me. He sat.

I glanced at Eyke. 'Do we have a tape-recorder?'

Eyke rose and left the office. I turned my back on

65

Selly and employed the interval in filling and lighting my pipe. Eyke returned with a small Grundig which he placed on the desk and plugged in. He tested it. It played back crisply. He placed the mike beside Selly and resumed his seat. Selly sat scowling at the recorder, at me.

'Look – I don't go much on this!'

'It's a time-saver. Yours will be a long statement. We can make the transcript from the tape.'

'It isn't bloody evidence, you know that.'

'It isn't intended to be evidence.'

'If I liked, I could have a lawyer!'

'Do you feel you need one?'

'Oh, stuff it.'

He glared for a while, then foraged in his pocket and came out with a cigar. He grabbed my matches off the desk and lit it and puffed smoke in my direction. His eyes scowled through the smoke. I took a few puffs and started the recorder.

'Where were you on Tuesday, then?'

'I was working for my effing living.'

'In Castleford?'

'Don't be wet. My territory runs from Grantham down to Harlow.'

'Including Wolmering.'

'So what about it?'

'Were you in Wolmering on Tuesday?'

Selly crowed scornfully. 'You have to be kidding. Where would I find a customer in this dump? I represent a manufacturing chemist, not an aspirin-bottling factory. Labs, hospitals, doctors, researchers and one or two big wholesalers. I'm half-a-bloody chemist myself, not a knocker who goes round chatting up the drug stores. My nearest customers are in Eastwich.'

'And that is where you were on Tuesday?'

'Suppose I was?'

I looked at Eyke.

'It's about thirty miles away,' Eyke said. 'An hour's run.'

'An hour's run. How long were you there?'

'What does it matter how long I was there! The point is I wasn't in flaming Wolmering, not how long I was somewhere else.'

'Were you there after six?'

'You get stuffed.'

'After eight?'

'Wet up your kilt.'

I blew a couple of puffs. 'I think you'd have spent the night there.'

His eyes popped. 'Drop dead. Drop bloody dead.'

I shrugged. 'Look what happened next day. You were beginning a journey to Scotland. But did you set off early, as most people would, to get a start before the traffic build-up? You didn't. You set off after lunch, and you were ready to call it a day at Harrogate. You'd done some driving already that day. You started from Eastwich, not from Castleford.'

Selly dragged savagely at the cigar. 'You're a clever, clever boy, that's what you are. I wouldn't have a lie-in Wednesday, would I, after my arseing-about the day before?'

'Why not? You could have had it at Eastwich.'

'Sod Eastwich. Crap on Eastwich.'

'We can ask Mrs Bacon.'

'You lay off Cathy!'

'It would perhaps be better to have merely her confirmation.'

Selly breathed quicker. His brow was glinting and now he was drooped a little forward on his chair. His eyes weren't on me but on the desk: rimmed, staring, searching the distance. Then they flicked back into focus.

'Now look – let's stop acting like bloody kids! We're on the same side, in case you don't know it. I want this bastard put away too. So what's the question – was I in Eastwich? Answer: yes, I sodding-well was! But I've got reasons why I don't want to broadcast it, and they've got nothing to do with Viv.'

'You stayed at a hotel?'

'No – yes!'

'Which hotel?'

He gestured with the cigar. 'You'd check, wouldn't you?'

'We'd check.'

'Yeah.' He took a bitter drag. 'So it wasn't a hotel. I've got a bint there. A bint that Cathy knows nothing about. And I don't bloody want she should know. Cathy's different. I'm going to marry her.'

'What is this woman's name?'

He hesitated. 'You wouldn't do the dirty on me, would you? I mean I can tell you to shag off, I've got nothing on my conscience.'

'It would mean us questioning other people.'

'I'll bet it would. You bastard.'

'I think you should tell me.'

He hissed smoke. 'You make it bloody plain, don't

you?' He jerked ash into Eyke's waste-can. 'All right. I'm stupid, I'll trust you. Her name is Jill Royce, Flat 7, 353 Wilby Street. She's divorced, works as a hairdresser. I picked her up in a pub one night. She thinks my name is Bobby Moore and I'm flogging adverts for directories.'

'Have you known her long?'

'Two or three months. I visit Eastwich once a fortnight.'

'Is she fond of you?'

'Fond of my dough. She wouldn't lie to the narks for yours truly.'

'Describe your movements, then.'

'Check. All day Tuesday I was in Eastwich. East Southshire General, Eastwich Labs, Shotley Chemicals, Reid and Murchison. Lunched at The Crown and Anchor, had a snack in Limmers later. Rang Jill. Met her at The Bull. Dinner, booze, home and bed.'

'What time did you meet Mrs Royce?'

'Around seven, or just after.'

'You were in her company all evening.'

'Right. And in bed with her all night.'

'Who else might have seen you at The Bull?'

Selly paused to huff smoke at me. 'Are you telling me Jill's word isn't good enough?'

'I would like the name of an independent witness.'

He puffed rapidly a few times, then pushed his shiny face closer to mine. 'You lovely so-and-so,' he said softly. 'You'd like to set me up for this, wouldn't you? But you can't, because I wasn't here. And you're never going to prove bloody different. So you can stuff your independent witness. Jill Royce is good enough for me.'

I fanned at his smoke. 'As long as you're happy with that.'

'You tell me why I shouldn't be happy.'

'You have just been telling me yourself. You had both motive and opportunity.'

'My Aunt Fanny!'

'Especially motive. You want to marry Mrs Bacon. Even with the new Act becoming law that was going to take you some time.'

'But shit, I could wait—!'

'Then there was the property, probably worth seven or eight thousand. And the continual drain of your wife's allowance, a matter of fifteen pounds a week. Any one of these three would provide sufficient motive. Add them together, and I think they will prove too much for the testimony of a Mrs Royce.'

'But Jesus Christ—!'

'Next, your running away.'

'I bloody didn't run away!'

'It was nicely timed. If discovery had been delayed your trip to Scotland would have made an alibi. Since it didn't, you had to make the best of things and return to pretend innocence, but why didn't you report straight away to the police? Was it because you needed time to brief Mrs Royce?'

Selly's breath was coming noisily. I had sweat trickling down his plump cheeks. He was paler, too, and his staring eyes had a bemused, straining appearance.

'You agree with me?'

He swallowed. 'You lousy bastard. What are you after?'

'Let's say co-operation.'

'Yeah. Yeah.'

He mashed the cigar in Eyke's ash-tray.

I gave him a rest. I switched off the recorder. Eyke sent out for some coffee. We left Selly drinking his in the office and took our own outside. Across a narrow street beside the station a fashion shop had built a patio, a square flanked on two sides by picture windows and with an acacia tree in the centre. Beneath the tree was a bench. We sat down there. It was sited to face the windows. Through the windows we could see slim, interesting girls dressed in svelte black dresses. A faint breeze ruffled the acacia and made patterns of shade around the bench. We drank our coffee silently for a while. The only foreign sound was of distant traffic. Then Eyke turned to me.

'What do you think, sir?'

I lifted my hand and let it fall.

Eyke nodded seriously. 'That's how I feel, sir. We don't have quite enough yet.'

'It's not that so much,' I said, sipping. 'But he was right, I'd love to pin it on him. Which is why I'm telling myself to be careful, to check all the factors he perhaps doesn't fit.'

Eyke considered his cup. 'It's a fairish case, sir.'

'You like him?'

'I think we could make it stick. His tart won't be much of a problem. I fancy Eastwich can wrap her up for us.'

'But the man himself?'

'I'll go along with him, sir.'

I shook my head. 'That's where I'm not certain. He's just a shade too sure of himself. I can't tell yet if it's genuine or not.'

Eyke looked disappointed. 'We've heard a lot of them bluster, sir.'

'Also, he isn't quite square with the picture.'

'With respect, sir, we don't know all the picture.'

'So that's another reason for being careful.'

Eyke was silent for a few sips. 'Then we won't be taking immediate action.'

'Not as I see it. But send your best man to Eastwich and get that alibi checked out.'

'What about his car?'

'Car and dabs. We're taking no chances with Selly.'

Eyke finished his coffee sombrely and we returned to the office.

Selly was standing by the window when we entered. He'd removed his coat and hung it over a chair. He looked cooler, warier, perhaps more respectful: a man who'd taken time out to do some thinking. Eyke shut the door and he and I sat down. Selly came across from the window slowly. He didn't take his seat directly but stood by it with his hand resting on the back.

'Am I allowed to say something?'

'You're quite free to.'

'Fine. I'd like to get something straight. I realise I've put my effing foot in it, and I don't blame you for thinking the way you do.'

'Thank you.'

'But I bloody mean it! I know my neck is sticking out a mile. The way you were putting it together the jury wouldn't bother to leave the box. Fatsy the patsy – that's me, and I'm telling you I appreciate that. But just the same it doesn't add up. I didn't have any reasons for killing Viv.'

I started the recorder. 'Why not sit down?'

Selly lunged forward suddenly and reversed the switch. 'Let that sodding thing be! I want to talk to you. Can't you listen without those spools turning?'

'Still, sit down.'

Selly sat down. He dragged the chair close to the desk. He leaned his elbows on the desk-top and scowled at me over the recorder.

'For a start, there's Cathy.'

'Have you changed your mind about wanting to marry her?'

'No! But it's a personal matter – just between her and me, compris? Us getting married isn't going to change anything. We're living like man and wife now. I wasn't sweating on a divorce – that could happen in its own good time.'

'And Mrs Bacon was satisfied with that?'

'If you don't believe me you can ask her, can't you? If it bothered her living with me without being married she'd have changed her name before now.'

'Is she well-off?'

'She isn't a pauper.'

'About how much?'

'You make me sick! She's got some property, two or three houses. But I didn't kill Viv to get hold of that.'

'All the same, you will stand to benefit.'

73

Selly glared, his hands clenching. 'The point is you can't make Cathy into a motive, and she's all you've really got against me. The rest is pathetic, bloody pathetic. I couldn't care less about Viv's allowance. I'm pulling in seventy, eighty a week plus an expense account and car allowance. So where does the big hardship come in? Do I look as though I'm counting coppers? If you're doing as well as I am, mate, you'll know the bloke to murder is the tax-man.'

'Your wife's allowance could have helped to pay him.'

'Except that single men are taxed higher. So it cancels out, and what you're overlooking is I never grudged Viv a penny of her money.'

'Nor the cottage.'

'Nor that either! I'd have made that bloody thing over to her. Viv was a feeble, half-cock bitch, but I owed her that much, and she'd have got it.'

'Then what you're saying is I don't have a case.'

'I'm saying your bloody motives won't stand up.'

'So all you need to show now is lack of opportunity.'

His eyes widened eagerly. 'And I can do that too. Listen, there's a waitress at The Bull called Rita, a sexy bitch with big titties. I've kidded her along once or twice, so perhaps she'll remember seeing me on Tuesday.'

'Did she serve you?'

'No. Our waitress was a mousey bit, one I don't know. But Rita was there, and she must have noticed me. And we didn't leave The Bull till after nine.'

I rocked my shoulders. 'Why didn't you mention her before?'

Selly gestured with his head. 'I wasn't trying, was I?'

'But you are trying now?'

He glanced at me sharply, opened his mouth, said nothing.

'Good. We'll leave that for the moment.' I started the recorder going again. 'What I want now is a little background. Tell me first how you came to meet your wife.'

He scowled at the recorder. 'That's bloody simple. We both worked for the same firm.'

'She worked for Corstophine?'

'Don't be stupid. Viv was never out of Brum. I was with Aplan, Rayner in those days – Atherstone Road, Solihull.'

'They were manufacturing chemists too?'

'That's my speciality, isn't it? I was their rep for South Wales: Swansea, Cardiff, Newport, the lot. Then they went bust and I joined Corstophine, but that was after we were married. A.R. got caught with thalidomide. I could see the crash coming so I cut loose.'

'What was your wife's job?'

'Typist. She was working in dispatch when I met her.'

'She was living with her parents?'

'She didn't have any parents. She was illegit, they'd dumped her in a home.'

'Why did you marry her?'

'That's a bloody good question.' He linked his short, hairy fingers together. 'I'm effed if I know. It couldn't have been sex. She had no more meat on her than a greyhound.'

'You were in love with her, presumably.'

He writhed impatiently. 'Not the sort of love you read about in *Peg's Paper*. She was rum . . . different. You couldn't figure her. What was going on behind that face.' He dragged on his fingers. 'Perhaps that was it. I wanted to find out what she'd got. The mystery bit: she hooked me with it. Something she had and the others hadn't.'

'Did you find out what it was?'

He laughed harshly. 'A bloody great empty nothing, mate. It was just a trick she had of holding herself back. Once you got past that there was nothing to her.'

'Yet you lived together for two years.'

'Maybe it took me that long to find out.'

'Was she a good wife?'

'That depends, doesn't it?'

'Were there rows, trouble?'

He shook his head. 'In a way she was a grateful bitch. I reckon she'd had a tough time. She tried. She didn't want to cross me. She didn't raise hell about other women. I gave her good house-keeping, personal money. She kept the house nice, fed me well. It might have gone on a hundred years, but hell, it wasn't marriage. We were just bloody strangers.'

'Then why did you separate?'

Selly hitched at his fingers. 'In the first place I met Cathy. She's a receptionist at the Castleford General, a real woman: the one I've waited for.'

'And in the second place?'

'Are you kidding?' He gave me a leer over the fingers. 'I came home one day and caught them at it. I couldn't touch her after that.'

'Who was with her?'

'Two bints from the school. I didn't ask for introductions.'

'Was one a red-head?'

'One was fair. The other was darker, sallow-looking.'

'What did you do?'

Selly parted his hands suddenly and made a popping sound with his lips. 'Kaput. I grabbed a few things and hit the trail. I haven't been back to Wolmering since.'

I nodded, eyeing him. 'Now let's go back to the time when you switched employers. You were appointed to this district by Corstophine. What made you choose to live in Wolmering?'

'It's handy for the job. Pretty central.'

'Surely not as central as, say, Abbotsham?'

'Abbotsham isn't on the coast, mate. We wanted a place by the sea.'

'You had been here before?'

'Never even heard of it. I rang some estate agents in Eastwich. They gave me half-a-dozen addresses, and this was the one with a sea view.'

'Had your wife been here before?'

'If she had she never mentioned it. But it's bloody unlikely. Rhyl or Blackpool would have been more in Viv's line.'

'So you bought the cottage and settled in. You began to make a few friends.'

Selly's eyes flickered. 'That's what you say. You can't have seen much of Wolmering yet.'

'But you had to be acquainted with a few people.'

'Oh sure. I called the butcher Fred. Then there was

the milkman and the paperboy. And the buster who read the meters.'

'Didn't you join anything – say the golf club?'

'Squire, I didn't even try. After I'd looked the natives over I decided Wolmering was just where I slept. They weren't me, compris? And I wasn't going to spend much of my time in the town. This place is just a bloody side-show, a lurk for the Old Folks at Home.'

'But your wife was here all the time.'

'True. But Viv was no mixer.'

'Neither she nor you made a single acquaintance?'

He spread his hands. 'That's about it. If we wanted a show, a meal, we used to slip into Eastwich. What knocked me most about the girls was that Viv had ever managed to pick them up.'

'You saw them just that once.'

He nodded.

'It was a surprise to you.'

'You're not kidding.'

'Then if she'd concealed that acquaintance from you, isn't it possible she had concealed others?'

Selly scowled. 'I'm not saying it isn't, but I'm bloody sure I don't know who they are. Look, I've been trying to tell you, Viv wasn't an easy person to read. She was a quiet, broody sort of bitch, never let much past her face. I didn't really know her, that's the truth, and in the end I didn't want to. What I did know shook me: there could have been plenty more.'

'And you can offer no suggestion?'

'No. But you'd better start looking further than me.'

I stared. 'We never stop looking.'

His eyes were tight. I stopped the machine.

CHAPTER FIVE

*F*RIDAY, *SHORTLY BEFORE lunch*. I did what I should
have done earlier: inspected the aspect of the town
as it faced towards the Common. I drove down over
the Town Green to the T-junction at the bottom,
made a sharp turn right and cruised at a walking pace
along the boundary road.

The first stretch included the car park, which
was simply a wide verge shaded by oak-trees. The
houses opposite were the end houses of two streets
connecting with Town Green: Georgian, meaning
they hadn't been provided with an outlook towards
the rude country. A hedge divided road and car park
from the Common but it was breached by a stile and
several gaps, from which departed tracks through the
shag-grass and thickets of yellow gorse. At this point
the Common swelled gently so that the view was not
extensive, but the gorse gave the impression (quite
illusory) that beyond stretched a tangled and perhaps
impenetrable wilderness.

The road climbed. Within a hundred yards you
reached a more comprehensive view-point, and from

there you could see the clean sweep of the Common and its smooth decline to the marshes. It was open and grassy, with shallow undulations and only occasional islands of gorse, stretching westward an indefinable distance to a vague conclusion of trees. Northward the fringe of trees was closer, and among them one saw the pale walls of the school; and further right the plebeian roofs of the houses outside the town. The road to the upper harbour, bumpy and unfenced, crossed the foreground of the scene, passing a concrete water-tower (a discordant feature) and, lower down, a modest sports pavilion.

I cruised further. Now the style of the houses was changing. By their witness, it must have been early in the present century when Wolmering began developing fashionable pretensions. First a small, then a large half-square of terraces passed on my right, architecturally complex and embellished with every ornament of *art nouveau*. The effect was pleasant. They were scrupulously maintained. Each barge-board and dormer was fat with paint. Near the angle of the larger half-square stood a crisp granite church with a rectory of the same style and material adjoining it. And these houses necessarily fronted the Common: they had been sited, with just that purpose in view. Any one of the cars now standing before them could have been driven in a straight line to where we'd found the body.

The road bent sharply around the second half-square but the superior terracing continued beyond. It was cut by the road to the upper harbour, which was also my return route to town. I parked near the junction and continued on foot. The last half-dozen houses butted directly onto the Common. They would have rear access, with their garages behind them, but you stepped out of their front gates straight on to grass. They ended abruptly at an unpaved lane along which also the town's social line clearly ran: so that the last house presented the same blank wall to it as the Georgian end-houses did to the Common. Across the lane stood a red-brick cottage, hiding its clown's face behind over-grown shrubs; then a stretch of allotments, looking similarly neglected, and finally the decisive boundary of the creek. Practically, Wolmering's approaches to the Common were entirely occupied by the affluent and accepted.

Any lessons? I stood in the sun with the smell of warm grass in my nostrils. From here, from any point along the terraces, one could pick out the tuft of holm oaks with a pair of glasses. If Vivienne had died in one of these houses then the distance of the Common would be beckoning irresistibly to her murderer, offering ready concealment for the body without the risk of, say, a trip to the harbour. The far side of the Common had few visitors and the body might remain undiscovered for weeks. The murderer, whoever he was, knew nothing of the fisherman who used the Common as a shortcut to the harbour. This man, Wicks, had been cycling home from a night-fishing soon after dawn on the Wednesday morning, so that Eyke, receiving a call from him, was at the scene only a few hours after the body had been placed there. But that could not have been anticipated: the murderer had acted free of this consideration: for him the Common must have appeared a safe solution, directly available, remote from witnesses. At one of those windows, now, he might be watching: seeing the detective standing in the sun.

And if this were so, our murderer had emerged a few more steps from his shadows. He was, or passed for, a man of some substance, of good background and education. He was probably married, because he had vulnerability such as Vivienne could recognise and exploit; and he was very likely an older or retired man, with a standing in the community to lose.

If this were so!

Once more, I was venturing on the tightrope of logical probability.

Yet always, somewhere down the line, the guessing begins to fit the guessed.

Lunch at the Pelican. They had given me a table in one of the big windows. Comfortably seated, I could watch Wolmering go by just on the other side of my plate and napery. At this hour the elite had retired to leave their High Street to shop-girls and visitors; and they must have been frying down the road, because the girls kept passing with newspaper packets. Soon this traffic ceased too, and the little market-place fell quiet. Out there it was a splash of brilliant sun, in contrast to the polite gloom within.

I drank my fruit-juice and quizzed the customers. Across the room I could see Selly. He was sitting at a table with a smartly-dressed woman who I assumed was Mrs Bacon. She was tall and lean-featured but she had large, calm eyes; Selly was chatting busily to her and she was listening silently, without change of expression. Then, still without change of expression, she looked at me, and Selly broke off to dart me a glare. She turned away. Selly muttered something quickly and began shredding a roll into his soup.

I smiled to myself. There were other lunchers who appeared to be finding my presence interesting. I caught the eye of a thick-set, blunt-chinned man who sat with his lady at a table to my left. He was about sixty-five and had a fresh complexion and hair worn *en brosse*; he tried to stare me down, and when he failed, screwed a gold-rimmed monocle into his right eye. His companion, straight-faced, her hair rinsed blue, gave me a hard look before turning her shoulder. Then there was a solitary luncher who smiled: it took me a moment to place him as the painter, Reymerston. He was wearing a grey tussore jacket and a pale green shirt, and nobody now would mistake him for a fisherman. He nodded towards a table near the service door. There sat two gentlemen angling for attention. One wore a bright mauve shirt, one a bright pink shirt; but I failed to see them. The Press.

Lunch proceeded. I had the plaice, followed by stewed raspberries and cream, and Gruyère. Excellent; I didn't hurry myself. The dining-room was empty when I rose. Across the hall, in the lounge, on a mock-Regency settee in the bow-window, I took my coffee and graciously conceded a pseudo-statement to the two reporters. Selly and some of the others had come into the lounge also, but they were sitting at a distance. Reymerston was there, taking cognac with his coffee, and the monocled gentleman (though not his wife). I saw off the reporters and poured more

83

coffee. I was watching Selly in my peripheral vision. He was talking to Mrs Bacon in a lowered voice and occasionally favouring me with a sharp glance. Reymerston, too, I caught studying me amusedly, but the monocled gentleman was gazing into his cup; so I was taken unawares when suddenly he put the cup down firmly, rose, marched stiffly to my settee, ducked his head, and sat. We observed each other for a moment or two. He put the monocle in his eye.

'Sir. Aren't you the fellow they've brought down from London?'

I nodded and murmured my name.

'Major Rede, sir. Late of the Borderers.'

He shot out his hand. I felt compelled to take it. He administered a brisk pump, at the same time staring into my eyes as though searching there for a secret sign.

'Any connection with the Berkshire Gentlys, sir?'

'If so I am unaware of it.'

'You have the features, sir. Our old Colonel was Lionel Gently, and he had the same cut of the jib.'

'But I know of no family ties with Berkshire.'

'I find that very odd, sir. I'd say there was kinship somewhere, if you took the trouble to make it out. Had you heard of the Colonel?'

'No.'

'He was a very charming fellow. People sneer at the term these days, but the Colonel was a true gentleman.'

I inclined my head.

'In the best sense, sir. It showed in his handling of a tricky situation. Always seemed to know the right thing to do, the proper course of action. The men loved him. And you're the same stamp, sir; I was telling my lady wife at lunch. No doubt why you were sent along. There are still a few up there who know what they're doing.'

I bowed again; the Major nodded sternly.

'And you agree, sir – the situation is tricky?'

'Of course, we'll try to be tactful.'

'The very word, sir. Precisely the word the Colonel would have used.' He gave his monocle an admonitory touch. 'Suppose you know my position in all this?'

'I believe so.'

'I'm *in loco parentis*, which is a very awkward thing to be. I daren't put the girl over my knee, though that's what she richly deserves. Daren't do it. She'd be off in a flash, and sharing a flat with some long-haired johnny. What do you do these days? The world's in a mess. I don't know what will happen to Pamela.'

'When did you learn of her acquaintance with Mrs Selly?'

'When, sir?' The Major's monocle glinted. 'Of course, I knew she'd taken up with the woman, her and her friends from the school. Never made any secret about it – they don't, you know, these days. Just look you in the eye and tell you they're going to the devil at seven.'

'You perhaps saw no harm in the association.'

'Aha, I don't know about that. True, it wasn't a fellow, but then it wasn't the sort of person I'd want a daughter of mine taking up with. Her husband had cut her, you know, and there's usually brimstone about then. And perhaps you'll call me a damned snob, but she had the speech and manners of a street-woman.'

'You knew her, then?'

'What? Well yes, I made it my business to. You can't stand *in loco parentis* to a young girl without vetting the friends she makes. Never actually met the woman, of course: I know how to be tactful too. Just asked a question here and there and took notice of what I saw and heard.'

'But you mentioned her speech.'

'I heard her talking in a shop. I entered the shop for that very purpose.'

'You were keeping her under surveillance.'

'No, I didn't say that, sir. My intention was to form an opinion of her character.'

'And you do that with all your niece's friends?'

The Major coloured delicately at the ears. 'I think, sir, you will allow this was a special case in which I had a duty to act as I did. Pamela's school-chums are unexceptional girls. They wouldn't be at Huntingfield if they were not. But Mrs Selly was a person of equivocal character and I had no hesitation in learning what I could about her.'

'You already knew her character was equivocal?'

'I knew she had been abandoned by the fellow down the room. And between ourselves I had observed him in the bar here, and I liked his character no better than hers.'

He sent a contemptuous stare towards Selly, who was now sitting alone, sullenly watching us.

'So you formed your opinion of Mrs Selly's character.'

'Yes sir. She was singularly worthless.'

'Then what do you think attracted your niece to her?'

'I think that woman set out to seduce her.'

'Have you grounds for thinking so?'

The Major's cheek twitched. 'She was a bad one. It was written all over her. Not safe with a man or a woman. Just had to look at her and you could see it.'

'You could see what?'

'Well . . .' His hand lifted. 'Something they have . . . an air. Like a cat's. Feel you just have to stroke them and they'll be all over you, anything you like. Sort of sweating temptation.'

'She wasn't physically exceptional.'

'Not a bit. She didn't have a figure a man would look twice at. But the way she held herself . . . moved. As though she was living it all the time.'

'A fascinating woman.'

His ears reddened again. 'In my opinion she was a whore, sir. And for what she did to those innocent young girls I would have had her flogged and put in a bridewell.'

'What did she do with them?'

He pulled up, staring. 'I don't think I have to tell *you*, sir.'

'But you knew?'

'Yes sir, I knew.' He grabbed at his monocle, twisting it deeper. 'No mystery about that. I began to suspect something. Way our girl was looking, behaving. So I asked her straight out what was going on. Do you think I'd hesitate to get to the bottom of it?'

'You asked her – and she told you?'

'Yes sir – she told me.'

'When did this interview take place?'

'It is enough, sir, that it did.'

'I'm afraid I must insist on knowing when.'

The flush had extended from the Major's ears and now he was gazing at me with watery eyes. The monocle dropped: he jammed it back again. Selly, in the distance, was following each move.

'Very well, sir. It took place recently.'

'As recently, say, as Monday?'

'It may have been Monday.'

'Was it Monday?'

The Major grunted and lowered his gaze.

'So on Monday you knew, you took some action.'

'The action I took, sir, was to forbid it.'

'Warning your niece, no doubt, that if she continued to see Mrs Selly, she would have to face unpleasant consequences.'

The Major jiffled. 'That was between us, sir. The details do not concern you. I did, I said what the occasion required for the proper protection of my niece.'

'On the Monday.'

'As you say.'

'Yet on the Tuesday her visits continued as usual.'

'I – well! I imagine she went, sir, to inform Mrs Selly that the business was over.'

'That is not what she says, Major Rede.'

'I assure you, the visit would not have been repeated.'

'Then I am to assume you took some subsequent action?'

The Major broke off. He'd begun sweating, like Selly.

I poured myself some more of the now lukewarm coffee and drank a couple of unhurried sips. Selly wasn't the only observer of this encounter. Reymerston remained at his table next to the wall. He wasn't watching us directly, but sat smoking a cigarette – a Russian blend: I could smell it – yet his table was near enough to the settee for him to catch a few words of what was passing. Otherwise there was only a waiter, who was collecting crockery down the room; though interestingly enough, he was the witness who had remembered Vivienne's visits to the bar. But he was paying us no attention, simply going about his business. I lowered my cup. The Major had stayed silent. He was staring at a point somewhat below my chin.

'I'm sure you will understand I need to ask you a few questions.'

He gazed at me wretchedly, then away. The flush had gone a little from his florid cheeks, on which appeared a few broken veins. But sweat still stood over his eyes.

'Which is your house?'

'Number one, Heathside.' He spoke in a lower, duller tone.

'That's the house on the corner of the larger green.'

'Yes, sir. Facing the Common and the green.'

'Were you at home on Tuesday?'

He made a little head-motion. 'Drove the lady wife into Eastwich that morning. Afternoon, in the house. I was writing a letter to Brother Frederick.'

'And in the evening?'

'Went for constitutional.' He eyed me defiantly. 'On the Common. Every evening for six years. Out at seven, back by eight.'

'Exactly where on the Common?'

'Golf Club. Stopped for a word with the greensman. Then round the gorse and home by the water-tower. Watched the goggle-box. Went to bed.'

I nodded. 'Did your wife watch the television?'

He gave me a sharp look. 'She wasn't in, sir. The lady wife has her own affairs. She takes a meeting on the first Tuesday.'

'However, there would be your niece?'

The tell-tale red had returned to his ears. 'My niece was out too.'

'Your niece was out . . .'

He stared at me angrily, his cheek twitching. 'There had been a row, sir. Something was said to which my niece took exception. The girl cleared out. Took her car. Didn't see her any more till bedtime.'

'What was the row about?'

'A private matter.'

I grunted. 'Let me do some thinking aloud. In the afternoon you wrote a letter and you may have gone into the town to post it. At about that time your niece and her friends would be leaving Mrs Selly to drive back to the school. You could have seen them leave, and so you would have known that your niece had disobeyed you – flagrantly and openly, the day after your alleged prohibition.' I paused. 'Or was it the day after? Was the matter not raised between you till Tuesday?'

The Major's monocle fell. 'Sir, this is impertinent.'

'In fact, was it raised by you at all? Wasn't it rather

your niece who brought it up, following some suspicion she had formed on Tuesday?'

'I shall not answer that!'

'Then we'll suppose it's the case. There was no talk, no admissions, no ban on the Monday. Yet you did take the action which your niece suspected, from which it follows you knew what was happening at Mrs Selly's. And the question is, how did you know? Who could have been your informant?'

'I have given you my account, sir!'

'And I'm not convinced by it. I don't believe in a confession by your niece.'

'It is true. My niece did confess.'

'But prior to the row on Tuesday?'

The Major jammed his monocle home, staring, saying nothing.

'You have nothing to volunteer?'

'No sir.'

'I would be sorry to draw the wrong inference.'

'That is your affair, sir.'

I nodded. 'We'll leave it, then. Tell me now, in detail, about Tuesday evening.'

He drew back, his eyes emptying, his bluish lips beginning to quiver; but before he could speak the swing doors parted and his wife entered the lounge. She saw us, paused, then came forward. The Major grunted his relief and rose. I rose also, though reluctantly. Mrs Rede gave each of us a tight smile.

'Please don't let me interrupt you. I came to tell Herbert I'd finished my phone call.'

She was a sturdy woman with a stubborn chin and analytic hazel eyes.

'Not interrupting, my dear. We'd finished.' The Major shot me a pleading look.

'Introduce us, Herbert.'

The Major complied. Mrs Rede presented a firm, ringed hand.

'You are welcome to Wolmering, Superintendent. Though I wish your business had been different.'

'Been discussing it, my dear,' the Major said quickly. 'Thought I should have a few words with the Super.'

Mrs Rede made a face. 'Nasty. Unpleasant. That amoral woman should never have come here. End it quickly and quietly, Superintendent, and tell the reporters absolutely nothing.'

'Man must do what he's come for, my dear.'

'Naturally Herbert. He'll do his duty. But there are cases best swept under the carpet, and this ugly affair is surely one of them.'

The Major screwed at his monocle.

'I'm sure the Superintendent agrees,' Mrs Rede said.

I shrugged. 'We try to protect the innocent.'

'That's exactly what I mean, you dear man.' She opened her handbag and took out a card. 'There. We'd love to see you on a free evening. But just now Herbert is taking me to the dentist's, and we must really try to be on time. Are you ready, Herbert?'

'Ready, my dear.'

He didn't look at me again. Mrs Rede steered him by the elbow. They passed Selly; went out.

I stood in the window, watching: a red 3500 Rover emerged from the yard. The Major, who drove it, was staring ahead expressionlessly; his wife's face was turned towards him, her lips busy. Was I on the mark? The Major fitted my diagram. I had little doubt now that he had written that letter. He had known; and not from Pamela, nor from the other young culprits. His information had come from Vivienne, because it could have come from no one else. And Pamela, she had guessed immediately that he was the author of the letter, implying she knew or suspected an acquaintance between her uncle and Vivienne; she had come home on Tuesday in a flaming temper to accuse and perhaps threaten him (I'll tell Auntie, I'll tell everyone, if you try to stop me seeing Viv). What then? Had Vivienne rung him, adding her threats to Pamela's? Had her desperate measure been a plan to confront him in his own home, before his wife? Then she would have found him alone, with a desperation matching hers, and what did happen could have happened, during the long empty evening. A little proof, and we had a better candidate than the man seated down the room . . .

I smelled exotic tobacco. Reymerston had joined me at the window. His eye met mine with a faint twinkle, though his expression was rather forlorn. A handsome man. He wore his hair in a careless lick, coming below his ears; but this suited him and made a frame for his large, spare features. He was tall and rangily-built. His age, around fifty, seemed a sort of prime in him.

'I overheard some of that, you know.'

'Then perhaps you'll keep it to yourself.'

He grinned. 'The Major isn't my style, but I

wouldn't want to spread scandal about him. On top of which . . .' He made a rueful mouth. 'I think his character rules him out.'

'You are an acquaintance of his?'

He drew smoke and let it trickle from his large nose. 'Nothing like that. I've chatted to him once or twice, in here, on the links. He's a bit of a blimp, but I think he's genuine. Perhaps he does have an eye for the women. But he lives by his code, that's my feeling. It would probably chuff him to have to take some medicine.'

I was startled. 'That's an acute observation.'

Reymerston grinned again. 'I'm a bloody painter. Full of secret, subversive judgements. If you need a spy, come to me.'

He stubbed his cigarette, nodded and turned to go.

'Wait,' I said. 'About last night. What made you jump in after the dog?'

'Oh – that.' He laughed. 'It seemed a pleasant night for a swim. The dog was there as an excuse, so I just took it and jumped.'

'Didn't the danger bother you?'

'There was no danger. I'd been on that swim before. You pick up the coastal current half a mile out. It fetches you ashore at Mindersley beach.'

'But why didn't you tell me that at the time?'

'It would have spoiled the moment,' he laughed. 'But thanks for sending out the boat – it saved me a tramp in wet clothes.'

He went, ignoring Selly's scowl; and I thoughtfully filled and lit my pipe. In a way his judgement confirmed mine: I too felt a twinge of uncertainty about the Major's character. If he were faced with disgrace, would his reaction be violence? I couldn't persuade myself of that. Or perhaps what I could see was his stocky figure depending from a rope or collapsed beside a gun. The violence would be turned against himself if it ever came to violence; but what was more likely was what Reymerston suggested, that disgrace would offer him a secret thrill. Shame to some is an erotic emotion, and the Major could well be one of these.

I puffed, watching Reymerston pass by the window. Twice this intriguing man had surprised me. He was an unpredictable element in this fairly predictable town. Now he'd gone I rather wished I'd held on to him: I sensed in him a key to some of my uncertainties. Plainly his spectrum of Wolmering was a wide one, stretching from the harbour-office to the dining-room of the Pelican. I had met him at the harbour: he could have been the man seen by Mrs Lake on Tuesday; and he had perhaps known Selly, however little sign he'd given of that a moment ago.

I glanced behind me, looking for Selly: but this time Selly's table was empty. Very silently, it must have been, he had slipped out; by accident or design, following Reymerston.

CHAPTER SIX

B Y ACCIDENT.
When I saw Selly next he was in the street
which led to Town Green, whereas Reymerston had
continued left, towards the promenade (I learned later
that he rented a beach hut near the Fishermen's Rest
Room). Nevertheless, Selly had raised my interest
by his stealthy exit from the lounge, and now I saw
him glance back furtively at the hotel as he hastened
along the pavement. Who was he trying to avoid –
myself, or Mrs Bacon? I lingered briefly at the lounge
window. Selly turned right, in the direction of the
Common, but nobody left the hotel to hurry after
him. Still watching, I knocked out my pipe; then I
left the hotel myself.

I didn't follow Selly, but crossed the High Street
and took a narrow lane opposite. This brought me
out at the top end of the Common car park, with
the smaller half-square of terraces to my right. I was
alert, and I needed to be. Selly came into sight at
the bottom of the lane. I faded behind a parked car
and watched through its screens as he glanced up the

lane, hesitated, continued. He was following the road beside the Common, just as I had done earlier, and I gave him plenty of time to get clear before I ventured to the end of the lane.

I came out of the lane warily, because here there was no cover; but Selly had kept going ahead and had vanished round the horn of the half-square. I moved up rapidly. At the turn in the road two benches had been sited on the clipped verge, and on one of them sat an elderly couple, sunning themselves, the lady with a book open on her lap. I chose the other bench, and sat; at the end nearest to the couple. If Selly glanced back now he would see this small group, but would scarcely be able to distinguish me from the others. In any case, he wasn't glancing back. His gaze was fixed forwards, at the houses in the terrace. At one particular house in the terrace: that belonging to Major Rede.

I sprawled a little on the bench so that I had a view past the lady's straw hat. Selly's businesslike strut slackened: he came to a stand before the house. He stood staring. The house looked lifeless. Strip-blinds were lowered in the downstair windows. A striped curtain hung in the rococo porch to protect the door from the sun. A slight darkness on the asphalt before the gate suggested the parking-place of Pamela Rede's Mini, but Pamela was at school, and Selly must certainly have heard Mrs Rede claim her husband to take her to the dentist's. Nobody at home, and Selly knew it. Why then his intent appraisal of the house? Was the fellow thinking (was it possible he knew?) that in this house his wife had died? His eyes moved over it, searching each detail of the ornamental bays and the squat dormers; the square downpipes, which a slim man could climb; the sashes, which a penknife blade could open. But housebreaking was scarcely in his thoughts either: there was nothing shifty in his scrutiny. Simply, he was taking it in, feature by feature, as though wanting to print it indelibly in his mind.

There were benches at the other angle of the half-square, also, and now Selly broke off his scrutiny to flop on one of them. I ducked a little lower behind the straw hat, but it was needless caution: his gaze was in front of him. His head was inclined forward: a man thinking. I could see a foot restlessly scuffing the grass. It was not so much the attitude of a person frustrated as of a person engaged in some complex problem. Selly was under pressure. His alibi was thin, and his story could be shot to pieces in court. What he needed urgently was – at least – a red herring that smelled enough to divide the suspicion with him. Though he couldn't have heard much of what passed in the lounge he could have read plenty from the Major's reactions, while if he knew the Major was related to one of the girls then he would surely have been putting two and two together. Certainly he knew where the Major lived, which inferred some previous knowledge of him. All in all, I decided Selly knew more than he had seen fit to admit to at the police station.

And now . . . what was his game? He had pulled out a cigar: was lighting it with quick, nervous puffs. He glanced aside at the house, at the Common, at us, making me sink my head forward. The time was two forty-five. There was little probability of the Redes returning for an hour or so, and when they did, what could Selly do? Having it out with the Major wouldn't get him very far. I paused in my thinking. Was I on the wrong tack – did Selly really see in the Major a heaven-sent red herring? I could think of another possibility: a relationship between them which the present crisis would enable Selly to develop. Yes: blackmail. All the elements were there, may even have been in train at an earlier date. Selly could have played the badger game with the Major, have been taking payments from him for some while past. It might be even that the Major had been coerced into maintaining Vivienne – a cheap way of settling a cast-off wife! – in which case Selly had now an irresistible persuader with which to confirm and extend his extortions. If the Major thought he had solved his problems by getting rid of Vivienne, Selly would very promptly disillusion him. One word from Selly to me and the Major would be booked for the assizes.

Yet – if this were the case – would Selly be hanging about here, waiting to make his approach in broad daylight? Staring at the house as though he meant to burgle it – irritable, puzzling, seemingly at a loss? Now he was drooped forward again broodingly, his cigar steaming from an angle: not a picture of a man who held all the cards and could play them when and how he felt fit. No, the pressure was there all right. Selly was in a mess and wanted a way out.

The lady had closed her book and was telling her husband she meant to pick up some cakes in the town: at any moment I would lose my cover and run the risk of Selly spotting me. I slipped out of my jacket, a grey light-weight, to expose the cream shirt I was wearing, then removed my tie and unbuttoned the shirt-front to give a casual, visitor-like effect. At the distance it would probably have been enough, but it wasn't immediately put to proof. Before my elderly friends could gather themselves together, Selly jerked away his cigar and got to his feet. He seemed suddenly to have arrived at a determination: he strode purposefully forward on to the Common. Very roughly, he was taking a line which would bring him to the holm oaks beneath which his wife's body had been found.

I let him go: I could do nothing else. There was no cover for some hundreds of yards. The nearest was the gorse scrub behind the golf-club pavilion, and Selly was between me and it. So I relaxed and watched him plod on his way while my lady and gentleman prepared to depart, each one favouring me with a dubious look which took in my wide-open shirt-front. They went: I resumed my jacket, but didn't bother with the tie. By now the distance was too great for Selly to have recognised me if he'd looked behind him – which he didn't. He'd changed his direction a little, to the right, and had crossed the road to the upper harbour; but this might have been only in order to pass behind the pavilion instead of in front of it. Patiently, I stayed where I was until his figure began to mingle with the gorses; then I rose and set off briskly on the shorter line to the pavilion.

It was warm on the Common, though there was a faint sea-breeze from the hazy bay to the south-east.

Now I was treading on short, gnawed turf and now wading through stretches of dusty tall grasses. I reached the road and the pavilion together; here I had to make a detour. On the other side, beyond the pavilion and gorses, the more remote and rough part of the Common stretched before me. It was more undulating, more scrubby, and included areas of bracken, ling and bramble; there were burns of gravel, and in the shimmering distance a faint reef of trees and a single dark smudge. The smudge was the holm oaks. Once more, it was impressed on me how fortunate we had been in the quick discovery of the body. In that far corner it might easily have stayed concealed until we searched the Common, perhaps weeks later. Because Vivienne might not have been quickly missed, or her absence have assumed immediate significance; the date, the time, the circumstances surrounding them, might all have been a closed book to us. I looked for Selly. There was cover enough now in the scrub and undulations and old choked pits, but unless he were deliberately concealing himself I must catch sight of him as he followed the line towards the holm oaks. I waited: no Selly, nothing that moved on the swart heath. Was it possible I had given myself away – perhaps hadn't been so clever, sitting on the bench?

When at last I did see him I silently cursed myself. He was far across to the right; it was my tidy mind which had been consigning him to the holm oaks. He had made no detour. His objective was clearly in the direction of the northern boundary. Now he was far away, perhaps half a mile off against the few hundred yards I had been anticipating. No need for cover!

I went straight after him, resisting a second attempt to cut him off. Unfortunately, at this distance, I was frequently losing sight of him among the thickets of gorse and the declivities. The tiny figure would vanish with mysterious suddenness, leaving the heathscape empty for several minutes, then reappear on an unexpected bearing to involve me in an arbitrary change of direction. Also – in spite of his overdressed plumpness – he was maintaining an energetic pace, so probably I was not gaining on him, and might even be losing ground. I laboured sweatingly across gravel and ling, down and up hollows, past clinging gorse; and still I had no idea where my far-off quarry was heading.

I arrived where he had been when I first picked him up again, and so in what must have seemed to him his most direct line. I checked back to the pavilion, then ahead into the heath: sure enough, I could see him directly in front of me. I looked beyond: a stand of tall trees: they closed the Common at its north-west boundary; for a moment I was baffled by the unfamiliar view-point, but then my mental map focused. Huntingfield School!

I brushed off some sweat and hastened forward again. This really was something I should have foreseen! Selly had pretended he hadn't known the girls, but he was a liar in every inch of him. If his wife had known them, wouldn't he have done? The girls, I remembered now, had half-conceded an acquaintance with him. And it might have been more than that. He could have been involved with one or other of them. For him, they might represent a source of information which would be obstinately closed to myself. He wanted to question them, but to do it secretly. He must know of some way to make clandestine contact. This long hot tramp to the rear approach of Huntingfield had to include a fair prospect of a meeting at the end of it.

I steered my course now less by Selly and more by the beckoning shade of the trees. It was impossible for me to reach them before he did but I wanted to be there at the first moment afterwards. Then, as I drew closer, I saw I was going to lose him; the foot-slope of the hanger was a jungle of rhododendrons; they formed a wide wild belt, advancing into the heathland, and stretching above to the pink shafts of a row of pines. I watched impotently. Selly approached them. His speck-like figure seemed briefly to waver. Then it vanished into the tall, dark bushes like an insect fading into long grass. Gone: I was reduced to dead reckoning, and any luck that might attend a deserving detective.

I marked the spot as well as I could and reached it five or six minutes after Selly. In the leafy mould beneath the rhododendrons I persuaded myself I could discern his footprint. But there was no path, and after a few yards I gave up my dubious tracking; just forged ahead through the hot dusty gloom and the whippy low twigs that seemed to favour face-level. I struggled up the foot-slope and emerged below the pines. Sky and bright sun showed dazzlingly beyond them. I could hear faint and irregular plunking sounds and a complement of distant girlish cries. I continued cautiously through the pines, through a belt of small birches, to a wall of yellow brick; and pulling up on this, I caught a glimpse of a playing-field with a number of soft tennis-courts at the further end. A tennis period! I hung on long enough to check that the players were upper-form girls. They were, and Selly had known they would be: his information about Huntingfield was significantly detailed.

But plainly I had not been following him by climbing the slope at the pines; I had been too eager. Selly had gone further, to make his approach near where the girls were playing. I hauled up again to study the layout. Along the left of the playing-field ran a wire-mesh fence. Outside this, more rhododendrons, a few of them still in bloom. Then, by the tennis-courts, and inside the fence, was a patch of variegated azaleas, beside which were three or four garden-seats on which girls sat waiting their turn to play. They were gossiping and laughing among themselves, and I could see no mistress in the vicinity; but what I could see was a flaming red head moving vivaciously and tossing backwards in mirth. Diane Culpho: if she were there, would the others be far away?

I dropped down and began to skirt the wall. It ended in a brick pillar with a ball on the top. Here the rhododendrons began again, but they had been planted hollow, with a path running between them. I moved along it as quietly as I could. The sound of the tennis-playing drew closer. Ahead, the neat lines of the rhododendrons had become confused and the path made a detour to the left. I negotiated the detour stealthily. Beyond was a small glade, with the rhododendrons thinning towards the wire fence; through a gap I could see the bright yellow, orange and blue of azalea blossom in open sunlight. The fence was unobstructed for a few yards at this spot, though shielded on the other side by the azaleas; and it was here Selly was standing, his fingers hooked in the mesh, with Pamela Rede facing him through the wire.

I dropped back to make a quick appraisal, but there was no way to get within earshot. They were fifty yards off. The little glade offered no cover, and I couldn't approach silently along the row of rhododendrons. I found a peep-hole and settled to watch. Pamela was facing almost directly towards me. A frail figure in a white tennis dress, she gave an impression of fearfulness, of vulnerability. She was shaking her head vigorously, her lips fluttering, and I could hear Selly's angry, aggressive tones; there was something a little bestial, a little ape-like about the way he clung to the wire. Once or twice she glanced over her shoulder, but Selly's growling voice snapped her gaze back to him; he exuded a magnetism which she couldn't escape: her slim form trembled but remained quiescent. He was growing angrier and dragging on the meshes. Pamela's head shook stupidly to and fro. Her face was pale, her eyes large, and I caught the tremulous denial of her tone. Then a woman's voice sounded authoritatively at a distance. The spell broke. Pamela ran. Selly was left wrathfully shaking the wire and calling after her in a threatening growl.

I came out of my cover and entered the glade. Selly heard me and turned, his face ugly. I walked up to him. I took him by the collar and sent him staggering some yards across the open space. He recovered and stood crouching, hands lifted, breath jerky and noisy, and I waited, praying, willing his attack, challenging the hate in his eyes. But he must have sensed it. Reluctantly, he controlled himself, dropping his hands and breathing lighter. I moved closer; I laid my hand on his shoulder and gave him a shove in the direction of the Common.

'You bastard!'

'Hold your tongue.'

I was keeping him moving at a sharp pace. We'd come down the slope through the rhododendrons and now I was prodding him across a stretch of heather-bush.

'Where are you taking me?'

'Don't you know?'

'You know I effing-well don't know!'

'So hold your tongue and keep moving.'

'I've a right to know—!'

I gave him a shove.

One incidental fact I had established which bore no reference to Selly: from the school there was no practical way of taking a motor-vehicle on the Common. The steep slope itself would have been a sufficient obstacle, but the tangle of rhododendrons made any such undertaking impossible; while even if a car had reached the Common the terrain in this corner would have defeated it. Miss Swefling was declining in the bill of suspects (though of course, the circumstances did not eliminate her).

'Look, I want to get back!'

'What's your hurry?'

'Because I'm cheesed-off with this bleeding common!'

'Something about it you don't like?'

He glared sweatily. 'Get stuffed.'

'I think you know this place,' I said. 'I think you've been here a few times before. You know enough to go straight where you want to go – which isn't where we're heading now.'

He spat. 'Are you going to pinch me for that?'

'It's a point I'm adding to a number of others.'

'Oh clever. And the answer is a lemon.'

'The answer begins at fourteen years.'

He spat again and I poked his shoulder. He was getting fatigued, which didn't grieve me. Over-many expense-account lunches and dinners were weighing down his hand-stitched, camel-skin shoes. We crossed two of the flat depressions and pushed through a belt of shoulder-high gorse; then, after another short struggle with heather-bush, we reached an area of scrubby grass and embedded gravel. The little clump of holm oaks was now close ahead of us. It consisted only of ten or a dozen trees. But they possessed in full that curious, self-intent animism which gives an uncanny aspect to a holm-oak. Haunted trees: they seem to watch you from another side of time. I marched Selly up to them. They grew in a rough square, as though planted there for some inscrutable purpose; at the east end was a gap, and we passed through it into the grove. Selly stopped just inside. It was dim and silent, with the dark-leaved boughs meeting overhead. He stared about, his eyes puckering. There were few signs to read in the dusty mould.

'Do you know where we are?'

'I can guess.'

'Let me see you walk to the other end.'

He just missed the spot where the body had lain, though whether by accident or design I couldn't decide. He mopped away sweat, scowling.

'Any use telling you I've never been here before?'

'No. You're too much of a liar.'

'It's bloody true, though. I haven't.'

'What were you doing up at the school?'

He found a sturdy low bough and sank on it wearily. 'So I know a bit more about the girls than I let on. You can't blame me for wanting to keep quiet about that.'

'How much?'

He leered moistly. 'I don't tell tales on the ladies. It was Viv's idea, to keep me at home. If you can't beat them, join them.'

'And you took advantage of it.'

'Wouldn't you?'

'No.'

'So you're a bloody saint, aren't you? And don't think they needed any pushing. That school up there isn't a nunnery, mate.' He dabbed at the sweat. 'But you're right so far. Kids like that aren't much fun. When I found them cutting it off with Viv it was all I needed: I blew.'

'And just now?'

'What about just now? I want some information, don't I? With a b. like you breathing down my neck and shoving me around for damn-all.'

I stared down at him: dripping, ugly, his eyes brazen with self-righteousness; then I broke a twig from one of the trees and began tracing an outline in the dry mould. Selly watched. The position may have been out, but I have an unfortunate familiarity with the shapes of bodies. When I finished it I could swear Selly was half-seeing the dead woman lying there in this chapel of trees. I tossed the twig away violently, making him start.

'What do you know about Major Rede?'

'Nothing.'

'You went to his house.'

'I was trying to figure—'

'How well do you know him?'

'I tell you I don't!'

'So what's your interest?'

'I haven't got any!'

'No interest. Yet you go to his house. Then you question his niece. You're a liar.'

'It's the truth I tell you! All I know is that you were rollicking him.'

His eyes were rounded (was there guilt in them?) and his mouth hung half-open. It was close in there among the trees: the mould smelled like stale urine.

'Very well. You don't know the Major. But you knew of his acquaintance with—' I stabbed a finger at the outline.

'But I bloody didn't!'

'You're lying.'

'I'm not! It's what I came here trying to find out.'

'And you did find out.'

'No!'

'You bullied it out of Miss Rede.'

'Ask her – bloody ask her! She swore blind there was nothing in it.'

'But you know there is.'

'I'm telling you I don't! It was you who gave me the idea.'

'And you liked it, didn't you? The Major has money.'

He scuffed at the sweat. 'Just get stuffed.'

I broke off another piece of twig and added some detail to my outline: hands, placed together on the breast, the way I had seen them in the photographs. The killer had been a respectful killer: he'd left the body decently composed. Even if he'd been a loving husband he could scarcely have killed and arranged the corpse with more tenderness. Selly's eyes followed the twig glassily. I could see him trying to moisten gummy lips.

'Have you sent a bloke to Eastwich?'

'Yes.

Again the tongue rasping his lips.

'Suppose no one remembers me?'

I shrugged, sketched a line to represent the chin.

'Look . . . give me a chance!'

'You want to confess?'

'No! But I'm not the bugger you're trying to make me.'

'So what sort are you?'

'I'm bloody human. Not a saint, but a human being. I never hated Viv, never wanted to injure her. I couldn't help it if we didn't click.'

'You're a liar.'

'All right then!'

'A bully. A whoremonger. You think it's smart to corrupt schoolgirls.'

'All right, all right!'

'Why give you chances? How many did you give the woman who was here?'

He stared at the diagram, his breath coming roughly. Now I had scored-in the division of the legs. A crude scrawl, as though someone had scratched a weak copy of a sepulchral brass: but the proportions were good. It was a woman who lay there in the dust.

'You didn't love her.'

He swayed his head.

'You felt your marriage had been a cheat. You resented her. She'd become an obstacle. She didn't merit any compassion.'

'It wasn't like that!'

'Wasn't it? With you neglecting her all the time? Would she have taken up with those girls in the first place if your behaviour had been less callous? And when she did, it was your excuse. You didn't try to understand her. She had taken a false step – fine! Now you could pack your bag and go.'

'But I never hated her!'

'How far off was it?'

He made a weaving motion with his head. 'You won't believe me, so what's the use? But I was fond of her in a way.'

'Not in any way that shows.'

'Because you don't want to bloody know! But we could be friends, a sort of friends. It wasn't all rows and putting the boot in. Just sometimes it was going for us. We could be pals, do things together. So it didn't last, didn't make a marriage, but it didn't make us flaming enemies either.' He jerked the sweat away

111

from his forehead. 'And what about me, my point of view? If I drove Viv into fooling with girls, didn't she drive me into chasing other women? We bloody tried, but it wasn't there. She knew, I knew, it was no damn good. I'm a whoremonger, right, but what made me one? Anyway, Viv could understand that!'

'Your wife connived at it?'

'She bloody did. Or else why did we stick together for two years? That was her way of making it up to me, letting me have a free hand. But it wasn't for ever, and she knew it. We were planning a split before the girls. She was getting the cottage and a good allowance – anything bloody callous about that? For all I know she set it up, letting me walk in on a session. I was dragging my feet, compris? She wanted to get shot of yours truly. So I went, and I didn't come back, but that didn't mean I didn't understand her, and I'm sorry now, bloody sorry, that Viv had to finish up like this.' He lunged to his feet. 'And you know something? I'm not just out to save my own skin. I want to find out who did it to Viv, I want to see that bastard behind bars. If it's bloody Major Rede I want to know that. I want to beat the sod into a pulp. Whoever it is I'm going after him. You'd better lock him up before I know.'

I grunted. 'You can depend on that. We don't permit private vengeance.'

'But you can't stop me asking questions, not with my own neck sticking out. You think you're a bloody fine detective and me, I'm just a stupid rep. But we'll see, mate, we'll see. I may be there ahead of you yet.'

I turned on him quickly. 'Does that mean you know something?'

'Me?' He sneered. 'What makes you think that?'

'What else did you ask Miss Rede?'

'Nothing that you wouldn't have thought of first.' He smeared his foot along the side of the outline. 'So I wanted to know about Viv's boyfriends. Who she was seeing, going to bed with. Things a husband likes to know.'

'And Miss Rede told you?'

'Told me nothing. Swore Viv wasn't having men.'

'What else?'

'Eff-all else. Some biddy called out, and Pam hooked it.'

I gave him a bleak stare. 'You won't be seeing that girl again.'

'Who says?'

'I say. Not her or any other of the girls.'

Briefly his eyes were dangerous, then he dropped them and took a kick at the outline. 'So you're the boss,' he said. 'Big man. You'll go to heaven when you die.'

'And you can forget about asking questions.'

'Why not lock me up now?'

'Because when I do it will be to keep you there.'

He met my eye, but said nothing.

I tramped-out what was left of the outline and motioned Selly through the gap. We headed back towards the town, silent, Selly a pace or two ahead. He turned when we neared the golf-club pavilion.

'Am I still supposed to be stuck with you?'

'You are free to go.'

'Thanks so much. Being seen with you helps nobody's image.'

113

He diverged to pass south of the pavilion, where some members stood talking near their cars. I continued to the upper harbour road. I saw no more of Selly at that time.

I fetched the Cortina and drove by the Major's house. No red Mini was parked before it. I proceeded to the school; there stood the Mini. I went up and knocked on the door of Miss Swefling's office. She received me icily.

'I hope this is not to become a habit, Superintendent.'

'My apologies. I am wondering if you will do me a favour.'

'Really?'

'I need to ask Miss Rede a couple of questions. You will help me very much by letting me ask them here, in your presence.'

She thought about it coolly. 'I take it this is nothing to the girl's prejudice?'

I met her eye. 'Not directly.'

'I see. You are very frank. And if I refuse?'

'Then I shall have to ask Miss Rede to accompany me to the police station.'

'In fact, I have no option.'

'I would sooner it was done this way.'

She allowed me some moments of her displeasure, then pressed a button on her desk. Pamela was fetched. She had changed back from her tennis clothes into school uniform. When she saw me she turned pale and swayed, and seemed half-inclined to faint; but she recovered and went to the chair which Miss Swefling had placed by her desk. She sat tremblingly. Miss Swefling touched her shoulder.

'Don't be upset, girl,' she said. 'The Superintendent is going to ask you some questions, but you needn't answer them if you don't want to.' She gave me a ferocious stare.

'Only two questions,' I said. 'First, did you tell anyone this afternoon that your uncle was acquainted with Mrs Selly?'

Pamela shuddered, her eyes dragging on mine, her face a white blur under them. Miss Swefling's arm tightened about her: Pamela's head began to shake.

'Second, were you aware of their acquaintance?'

Her eyes rolled: I thought she must faint. She felt for Miss Swefling's arm; then the motion of her head became a nod.

CHAPTER SEVEN

AT THE POLICE station I talked to Eyke, using him as a sounding-board for my ideas. He was predictable. As between Selly and the Major, his bias was all towards the former. It was almost like this: if the Major was the culprit, Eyke didn't very much want to know about it. Selly would do. There was a case against him, and the tidy thing would be to set it in motion. Eyke's man, Sergeant Campsey, had returned from Eastwich and his report by no means favoured Selly. The waitress at The Bull didn't remember him, and the prostitute, Royce, told a variant story. She'd had a meal with Selly at The Bull, but then she'd left to keep a date with a client. Selly, she supposed, had remained at The Bull until he rejoined her, at her flat, shortly before ten p.m. Thus Selly was covered by nothing that would raise doubt in the minds of the average jury. Meanwhile, Eyke's coverage of the Common houses had produced neither suspect nor information, so that, setting aside my inconvenient nominee, the ball remained firmly with Selly. The Major was mine,

Eyke gently insinuated; he and Wolmering wanted no part in him.

Selly . . . or the Major? I was trying to get a fix, an intuitive nudge, towards one or the other. Usually in a case I can find myself leaning towards one or another of the available alternatives. An essential faculty: there is too often a point where probabilities balance. Then you're on a plateau, and unless something is stirring beyond the bare facts you have come to a stand. And this time, apparently, nothing was stirring; I was being left aloof on my plateau. Could it be that I wasn't fancying either the Major or Selly, but was moving unconsciously towards some third solution?

At dinner at the Pelican I let my mind wander among the other possibilities, trying to discover if it was secretly finding a favourite for itself. It lingered awhile with Miss Swefling (who was undoubtedly my best outsider), but I was obliged to concede that this was due less to suspicion than to my good opinion of her. Not a criterion, of course. I have met several murderers whom I liked. If sympathy and antipathy were a fair test I would be happy to settle for Selly. No: what I was seeing in Miss Swefling was a blend of strength and generosity which even under pressure would resist the temptation to seek an answer in violence. For her it would be no answer, but an even less tolerable alternative. Scandal, personal disaster, she was equipped to meet, but not the self-judgement that would follow violence. I dismissed her and moved on into more remote country. The girls: they were closest to Vivienne; didn't instinct twitch a little there? Certainly three of them had returned to school, where they were supposedly confined during the critical period, but my knowledge of the school and its grounds suggested there was small certainty of this. They could have slipped out, to be met by Pamela, who had no precise alibi, and then have met Vivienne, perhaps by the Common, or even at the cottage if she had returned there. A possibility. And violence was already an element in their relation. Vivienne's body had borne no lash-marks, but there certainly would be shoulders that did. Had they turned on her, in a sadistic frenzy, and perhaps not realising what was happening to her? Holding her down, say, under a quilt, until the significance of her stillness horrifyingly registered? I kept this picture in my mind while I recalled my interview with the girls, trying to fit it to their attitude, the ring in each voice. But it faded. They were too poised. No horror of that sort was weighing down on them. With the insouciance of the young they were perhaps more intrigued than gravely shocked by what had happened to Vivienne. But what came into my mind now, in this connection, was the change in Pamela this afternoon. The poise had gone when she was talking to Selly and had become sheer panic in her encounter with me. The difference had to be Selly. Was Selly then a threat? To be seen talking to him a fatal circumstance? She too had lied about the extent of their acquaintance, though she might be allowed more excuse for that than Selly. I let myself dwell on the scene at the fence, the sharp image of the frightened girl: slim, vulnerable, large-eyed, looking younger than her age in the short dress. A person in shock: Selly had shocked her; had started some

118

unbearable line of thought; something new, which hadn't been there when I had spoken to her the previous evening. And directly I could hear his bullying growl and the crucifying words he'd thrown at her: Your bloody uncle did it, didn't he? And now I'm supposed to carry the can! The bastard. I could feel my hands clenching. But there was a corollary I daren't overlook. Why had his assertion seemed so devastating to Pamela unless it squared with facts already in her possession? She heard, she believed; in desperation she denied that her uncle was acquainted with Vivienne Selly. But when I had come, with my apparent omniscience, the admission had dropped from her like a ripe fruit. If I'd asked for more I would probably have got it; and of course, there had to be more.

So my soliloquy ended where it began. I rose and went to the call-box in the foyer. I rang the Major.

'Superintendent Gently. I'd like a few words with you this evening.'

A pause. 'Do you mean at the police station, sir?'

'No. You'll find me in the lounge at the Pelican.'

Another pause. 'Very well, sir. I will present myself in twenty minutes.'

'Wait,' I said. 'Is your niece at home?'

'My niece has gone up to her room. Did you wish to speak to her?'

'Not now.'

With luck, Miss Swefling would have repaired some of the damage.

Reymerston was sitting in the lounge and he greeted me with his quick smile. I felt an urge to go over and

119

talk to him: someone normal, a friend from outside. The case was riding me a little. I wasn't proud of what I'd done to Pamela. I didn't want to follow it up by trampling on her uncle and I hoped she didn't know I'd called him out. But I was a policeman: I gave Reymerston a tight grin and chose a chair near the doors. Reymerston shrugged faintly, looked a moment, then picked up a paper and ignored me.

I smoked a pipe. The Major arrived. He had taken five minutes longer than he'd said he would; he was spruce and smelling of after-shave lotion, but there was a flutter in his manner. He looked uncertainly round the lounge, which was filling up as dinner ended.

'Do we talk here, sir?'

I shook my head. 'I think we'll stroll round to the cottage.'

'The cottage?'

'Mrs Selly's cottage.' I took a key from my pocket and showed it him. He blinked at it.

'But . . . is that quite proper, sir?'

'Would you rather not go to the cottage?'

'No, of course! I was simply wondering . . .'

'I assure you it is quite in order.'

He gave his monocle a touch. 'Very good, sir. If that's the plan of campaign. But before we take this liberty with the dead, perhaps you will join me in a drink.'

I stared a moment, then shrugged. The Major preceded me into the bar. He ordered a brandy for himself, and I accepted a small Scotch. When they came, he half-made the gesture of touching his glass to mine, but then checked himself awkwardly and took a quick gulp instead. I drank silently. The waiter who'd served us was the one who'd made the statement about seeing Vivienne. I noticed him staring at the Major and myself and once he passed close to me. But he didn't say anything. The Major drained his glass.

'I'm ready sir.'

We went out into the quiet evening town, with the Major, who was almost a head shorter than I, bobbing along briskly, and punctiliously in step.

'The best time of the day, sir.'

I grunted. The shot of brandy was giving him Dutch courage. I wished the Scotch would do the same for me: I was less and less relishing the job ahead.

'Have you been to Wolmering before, sir?'

'No.'

'Most charming spot on the whole coast. Settled down here seven years ago. Never regretted it. Never.'

A little quiver in his voice. He was gazing ahead, not looking at me. Whatever had happened, back at the house, he must know that something critical had developed.

'This is my time for an evening walk . . . lovely air we have here. Sun lighting up the sea. Wouldn't want to change anything.'

'Do you always take your walks alone?'

'What? Yes. My own company. Lady wife a trifle lame, doesn't walk so far these days.'

'And your niece?'

He bobbed a few paces. 'Niece has friends of her own age, sir.'

'So it's always alone.'

'Sir.' He stuck his chin out, was silent.

We reached the green. I was walking outside him, and now I deliberately fell back. We passed the baroque house and its neighbour, passed the cottage adjoining Seacrest. He hesitated, partly glanced at me, then came to a stand at the right door. I took out the key and handed it to him. He unlocked the door. His hand was quivering. I ushered him in ahead of me, recovered the key, closed the door.

'Where to now, sir?'

'The lounge.'

This time the hesitation was longer. We were standing at the head of a long hall which led to an inner lobby and the kitchen and scullery. A door left gave access to a front room and there was a second door further along; to the right some graceful though narrow stairs rose steeply and turned on to a landing. I gave the Major a gentle nudge: he turned instinctively towards the stairs. Of course. The lounge was upstairs. Vivienne Selly had wanted to see the sea . . .

Again at the landing he chose the right door, though here it was a simple piece of logic. We entered a square, modest room of which the focal centre was its single sash window. A low coffee-table had been placed below it and the chairs and settee faced this direction. The furniture was good but not modern, suggesting that the Sellys had bought it with the house. A peaceful room: it smelled faintly of ciga-rette-smoke, and an unemptied ashtray stood on the coffee-table. I lowered the window. It admitted the soft whisper of the sea.

'Please sit.'

I remained by the window; the Major chose a chair at a little distance. He leaned back in it and tried to seem at ease, but appeared to have trouble finding a position for his hands.

'Now, please tell me what happened on Monday.'

'On Monday . . . ?'

'The day you wrote to Miss Swefling.'

'I! I wrote to her?'

'Do you deny it?'

His eyes avoided mine; his hands were wandering.

'You wrote a letter warning her against Mrs Selly. It contained information that proved to be correct. Presumably you came by that information on Monday – and it wasn't confessed to you by your niece.'

'Did Pamela tell you that?'

'What are you telling me?'

'I wish to know, sir, what my niece has been saying.'

'I suggest you ask her.'

'But I am asking you, sir!'

'And I am not obliged to give you an answer.'

His hands stiffened: the brandy was staying him; he had caught hold of an excuse for indignation. Pat on cue came his riposte:

'And I am not obliged to answer you either, sir.'

I sighed to myself. 'You don't wish to explain to me.'

'I am not aware I have anything to explain.'

'You would prefer that I act on my suspicions.'

'You, sir, may do . . .' He let the sentence trail expressively.

'Please listen carefully,' I said. 'I'm afraid your

123

niece is very disturbed. I think it is likely that she was unable to face you this evening. Frankly, I don't want to be forced into questioning her, and I'm hoping to find some way to avoid it.'

'I forbid you to question her!'

'You can't do that.'

'But I can forbid her to answer, sir. And what is more I can hire a lawyer. We don't have to submit to your persecution.'

'Exactly who will your lawyer represent?'

'We, us: my niece and I, sir.'

'I doubt if your niece will have much need of him.'

'Sir, I shall do what I think fit.'

Words boldly spoken. But his eyes missed mine, his hands were back to their old tricks. At this point, carrying it through, he should have stalked out, not remained weakly sitting to invite fresh attack.

'I think we'll go next door.'

'What . . . where?'

'Into the room adjoining this one. Naturally, certain items were removed for tests, but now they have been replaced exactly as we found them.'

His eyes were horrified, tremulous. 'Is this necessary . . .'

'Have you some objection?'

Unwillingly he shook his head. I moved from the window: he rose unsteadily.

Once more I made him go before me. The door of the bedroom opened on darkness. The window, a small one, had been hung with heavy curtains which fitted close and excluded all daylight.

'Switch on the light.'

His hand faltered, reached out. But nothing followed the click of the switch. It couldn't: the bulb had been removed, had doubtless been missing for many a day.

'No – the other light.'

'I – I'll pull the curtains.'

'The light please, Major Rede.'

I nudged him. He stumbled into the darkness. A little later, a dim red glow lit the room.

I closed the door. The light came from a table-lamp which had been swathed in a red fabric; it stood on a mantel-shelf opposite the door, and was barely sufficient to make the room distinguishable. In the centre was the bed. It was a low double divan with neither head nor foot-board, draped in red velveteen and furnished with a bolster and a number of cushions. Ropes of soft nylon were attached to each leg and the horsewhip lay among the cushions; bed and cushions were tousled and crumpled, and the tail of each rope had been formed into a slip-knot. Around the bed were placed three pouffes. There was a padded chair, also fitted with rope. The only other furniture was the tallboy, which bore the ashtray, dirty glasses and decanter of whisky. The air, though stale, had a powdery fragrance, and underfoot the carpet felt padded and springy.

The Major had stayed across the room. I could hear his thick breathing. He had turned his face away from the lamp: he appeared as a heavy shadow, gilded with crimson. I picked up the whip and flicked it, making the lash whisper over the bed. The Major's breath caught in a moan: he edged further towards the gloom.

'Was it . . . in here, then?'

I cracked the whip, making him jerk straight suddenly. His monocle had gone. Half his face was still shadowed: he stared wincingly at me across the bed.

'Is this your property?'

'I . . . I . . .'

'Better take it then!'

I hurled the whip at him. He threw up his hand too late and the stock caught him across the face. He grabbed the whip awkwardly, sobbing.

'Now, we'll make a fresh start. You were going to tell me what happened on Monday, why you wrote the letter to Miss Swefling.'

'You c-can't prove that!'

'You've just admitted it.'

'No!'

'Yes! Don't bother to lie. Or do you want me to rope you to this bed and flog it out of you – the way she did?'

'It's not true!'

'Hand me the whip.'

'Oh God. Oh my God!'

'You've been here before. You know this house. You know this room, all that went on here.'

'Please . . . no!'

'You were her lover – or she was yours. Which was it?'

'Please. . . please!'

'Hand me the whip.'

'No, no . . . oh no!'

He dropped sobbing by the bed, his face burrowing into the velveteen drape. It was obscene. I could have kicked him. I knew suddenly he wanted me to use the whip. I took a couple of steps to the window and flung the curtains wide apart, letting a blaze of evening sun fall on the moron snivelling at the bedside.

'Get up!'

'Oh, please!'

I grabbed his arm and yanked him to his feet. He blubbered and squinted, dazzled by the sun, but I wouldn't let him hide his face from it.

'Pull yourself together!'

'Please, please!'

'If you don't, I'll shove you under the shower.'

'You . . . you're heartless!'

He screwed up his eyes and sobbed.

It was enough: too much. I dumped him on the bed and got out of that room. I went back into the lounge and lit my pipe and stood staring through the window at the ships that passed.

Several did pass. As I smoked and waited I was watching the sun go out of the sea, and distant green hulls, buff funnels, white superstructures fade into blueness on a distant slate plain. At my elevation the horizon was remote, and never more so than during these minutes: the approaching night seemed to reveal a new country in the last narrow band between sea and sky. Ships, which before were simply larger or smaller, were now precisely charted in their relation with each other, and the high, pale curtain that

127

stretched from beneath the cliffs appeared as only a small step towards the vastness beyond. And watching all this I found myself switched off: as though I had stepped out of time for that while.

But time returned. I heard a step behind me. The Major stood in the doorway. He wasn't snivelling now, just looking pathetic, his monocle dangling and his eyes reddish. He had a glass of whisky in his hand: the glass was one of the dirty ones from the bedroom; they had been printed, but not washed, so he could have been drinking after his niece or the dead woman. I beckoned to him. He entered the room. Now I could see his face was paler. But there was a stillness about him, an absentness: perhaps the beginning of resignation.

'I suppose my . . . lady wife . . . must be told.'

I twitched a shoulder. 'This isn't a game.'

'It will be a shock for her, a great shock.'

'So will the news of your arrest.'

'But I'm not guilty, sir. That is the truth.'

'Then you have a great deal to explain.'

'Yes.' He closed his eyes and took a sip from the gummy glass.

'You'd better sit down.'

He moved obediently, taking a chair near me and the window. I sat across from him and occupied some moments in scraping out and relighting my pipe. Should I take him to the station? My instinct was against it. The delay and change of scene might break the spell. He was ripe now, ripe for confession, and once I'd got it I didn't think he'd go back on me. He sat stooping forward, his arms on his knees, his empty eyes fixed on the coffee-table. Give him a cue? No. I drew smoke silently, and waited.

'You . . . you haven't any personal experience, sir?'

I tried to get his eye, but couldn't.

'Experience of what?'

'Of . . . that sort of thing.' He gestured with his head towards the bedroom.

'I meet it in my profession.'

'That's not the same thing, sir. You're seeing it only from the outside. But it's different, sir, not what you'd think. Not . . . wrong. You don't feel that.'

'Is what you feel the criterion then?'

'Yes, sir. Yes. There can't be any other. Condemn me if you like – despise me, sir. But I don't condemn or despise myself.'

'Perhaps you feel superior to common morality.'

His head jerked. 'You don't understand. Morality and immorality don't come into it. It's something . . . beyond that. Something . . . loving.'

'You love the lash.'

'No! But a loving relation . . . a tender feeling.'

'Expressed in violence.'

He gave a dragging sigh. 'It wasn't wrong. It was a way . . .'

He drank some more, several sips, his hand and lips trembling. I looked away. The sea was slowly blanching as the night crept out from under the sky. The dull blue shape of a passing trader was dusted with a pale, secretive sparkle: lights. And the gentle surfing sounded hollower, more articulate.

'This . . . it's been going on for several months.'

'How did you come to make her acquaintance?'

'One evening . . . before that I'd noticed her sitting in the bar of the Pelican. Watching me . . . you know the way a woman makes a man notice her . . . then smiling. Something in her smile. Never anyone sitting with her.'

'Did you speak to her?'

'No. Didn't have the nerve to, sir. I mean, I'm pretty well known in there, it would get about if I talked to strange women. But I kept noticing her, the way she sat, the way she dressed, held herself. And her face, that was unusual. Had to keep wondering about her face.'

'In fact, she was laying for you.'

He sighed gently. 'Yes, sir. I have to admit that now. But at my age it is a little flattering to arouse even that much interest in a woman. She was young-ish, you know, could have gone for youngsters. Must have been something she liked about me. And she was good to me, never disrespectful . . . never till that one time.'

'How did she pull it?'

He was briefly silent. 'I met her one evening on the Common.'

'You mean she met you.'

'If you say so. She was merely exercising her dog. The dog was lame, sir – thorn in its foot – wasn't any doubt about that. So I took a look at it, natural thing to do. Then I helped her carry it back here.'

'That dog was permanently lame.'

'It was in pain, sir. I can vouch for it.'

'It was still lame yesterday evening.'

He drew a deep breath, but didn't reply.

'So she brought you straight here, into her parlour.'

'Yes sir. I've just admitted it.'

'Then the dog was forgotten. She gave you a drink. Told you how happy she was to make your acquaintance.'

'It wasn't quite so crude, sir.'

'But that's what happened?'

He nodded, his mouth bitter.

'And you finished up in there with the red lamp, and a tale to be told when you got home.'

He winced.

'What was the damage?'

'Sir?'

'How much were you paying Mrs Selly?'

'Paying her?' He looked startled. 'It wasn't *that* sort of association, sir.'

My turn to gape! 'You mean you weren't paying her?'

'No, sir. Money didn't enter into it. I gave her presents, cigarettes, a handbag, but never money. It would have been degrading.'

'But . . . what was she getting out of it?'

He coloured delicately. 'That is not for me to say.'

'It was pure love?'

'A loving relationship.'

'But with a whip!'

His mouth shut tight.

We sat silently again. I didn't believe him for one moment. Vivienne had been queer, but scarcely queer enough for a perverted love-match with a sexagenarian. Meanwhile, alongside, and doubtless more agreeable to her, had continued her antics with the girls; and it was against this background that she had set out to bring the Major into her clutches. An ulterior motive there must have been: had she been clever enough to conceal it? Unlikely, and so much more likely that the Major was simply lying. I stared: he moved uncomfortably; he nervously drank the last of his whisky.

'I want the truth! Are you claiming she asked nothing of you?'

His glass jogged. 'Not – not till Monday.'

'Not till Monday!'

'That was the only time. Until then she'd never asked for a penny.'

'But on Monday she did?'

He squeezed the glass. 'Sir, even then it wasn't what you think. There was a business matter she wanted help with. She could conceivably have gone somewhere else.'

'Except that you she could blackmail.'

His head drooped. 'There were . . . threats. She became excited.'

'Perhaps more than threats. Revelations?'

His head drooped further; he looked beaten.

'So now we're back there again,' I said. 'What it was that happened on Monday. Leading to what happened on Tuesday. And this time, I'd like the answers.'

Footsteps passed below, out of sight, and he cocked his head, listening. They faded. The room was isolated again by the sea. Out there the pallor and the darkness were merging into a uniform greyness, with the horizon no longer distinct between water and sky. Ships, moving jewellery, could have been sailing or flying in the undifferentiated void. A street-light flipped on. Its light was wan, ineffectual.

'You think that I . . . did it?'

'I think you had reason.'

He drew a deep, wavering sigh. 'Yes sir. Yes. Reason enough. I'd think the same if I were in your shoes. I'm a soldier, too. That's against me. I know all about killing. There's plenty of blood . . . here. I was at Alamein, sir. At Normandy.'

'You have killed men.'

He nodded. 'But I did it without hatred.'

'Still . . . you took life.'

'Not willingly, sir. Not to serve a personal end.'

'But the way is familiar to you.'

'I know too much, sir, to take that way. It comes back to me too often. It should be no man's duty to kill.'

'Yet the occasion arises.'

He sighed again. 'The poor girl. She must have been desperate. But it was no use. I couldn't help her. I simply didn't have the funds.'

'Then money did come into it.'

'Yes. But not as the prime consideration, sir. What she was seeking was an object in life, something to save her from aimless drifting.'

'And that was to be what?'

'A little business, sir. A shop in Church Street she had her eye on. She had noticed that we lacked a wool-shop in Wolmering and she was convinced she could make one pay.'

'With, of course, your support.'

He bowed his head. 'The project required a certain capital. The shop needed decorating and fitting-out, then there'd be the stock and a little publicity. But she wasn't asking for a gift, sir. The proposal was partnership. She had some small savings she was prepared to contribute. I would receive capital repayment from profits plus an adjustable income during the life of the partnership. It was sound: she had had business training. But unhappily, I didn't possess the capital.'

'So that was it!'

He ventured a glance at me, but quickly sank his eyes again.

'She was setting you up for a fat shake-down, and on Monday the pressure began. What were these threats?'

'She was excited, sir—'

'The first was to tell your wife, wasn't it?'

'Sir—!'

'And then to put it about the town that the gallant Major was a flagellant! A fine scandal. You'd be finished here, through with your wife, through with Wolmering. And on top of this a piece of news – your niece was in it as deep as you were!'

'Sir—'

'What was the end to be? How were you going to shut her up?'

'Please, I beg you!'

'You couldn't – could you? Because you didn't have the money!'

The glass clattered to the table and he covered his face and whimpered. I stood up, letting my chair scrape, and closed the window with a slam.

'Of course, you had to kill her. I understand that. It was the only practical solution. She forced it on you. If she'd been less greedy you might have worked something out. And you'll get sympathy. The people here didn't have any time for Vivienne Selly. All that really matters now is how to clear things up quietly.'

'No . . . no.'

'Yes. That's best. A defended trial would bring the press in. If you don't defend they won't be interested – it'll be just a walk-through at the local assizes. You won't be required to say a word, we'll simply read out your statement. A piece of routine court-business. Only good for a filler paragraph.'

'I can't . . . !'

'It won't really be so bad.'

'Please, no! Don't ask me.'

'It'll be off your mind. You can relax.'

He rocked his head. 'Can't. Can't . . .!'

I banged out my pipe on the stacked ashtray. Sick, sickening: a filthy business. And not even a confession to extenuate me, to let me feel I was a good policeman. I struck the table.

'All the same, you did it!'

'No sir, no. No, no!'

'You plumped a cushion on her face, then put your weight on it.'

'I am innocent, sir. Please, I am innocent!'

I stared down at the poor swine, but the disgust was for myself.

'All right. Get up. We'll take your statement.'

One way or another, I was going to ruin him.

CHAPTER EIGHT

B<small>UT NOT YET</small>: not quite yet. I permitted myself to do a foolish thing. Perhaps somewhere along the line the town had begun to soften me, to win me over on its side. At the station we found only two duty men: Eyke and his colleagues were out or off-duty; but on his desk still sat the tape-recorder, with a virgin spool newly-fitted. I used it. That was quite improper. Officially, I hadn't taken the Major's statement. All those damaging admissions, now docilely repeated, could be denied again as readily as uttered. I didn't think the Major understood this, but any lawyer he employed would; and if a case was lost in consequence it would be a serious blot on my record. To hedge my bet I put a seal on the spool and had the Major sign it before witnesses; but this was window-dressing. The spool was fiction, and only the Major could make it something else.

A fine evening's work! I returned to the Pelican to wash out my mouth with Scotch. The bar was crowded and droning comfortably with conversations I couldn't join in. I sat till closing, about half-an-hour.

Then the waiter I mentioned came to tell me his piece. He'd just remembered the Major's buying Mrs Selly a drink, a medium sherry, but several weeks ago. That one time? That one time. The Major, and nobody else at all.

I slept badly and woke when the shadows were still long in the market-place. I tried to drowse again but couldn't; I bathed and dressed and went down. The kitchen staff were stirring and they gave me a mug of their special brew: sweet, pungent stuff, about the colour of old mahogany. Then I went out. I went up by the Guns and along the low road to the harbour, striding briskly, trying to throw off the dull fumes from my brain.

Because I hadn't slept the Major away, nor the frightened face of Pamela Rede. The one and the other had broken my rest all the time my head was on the pillow. I was dreaming of hangmen, of the death-cell, of two collapsed figures being dragged along passage-ways: the ghastly dreams I used to have before state murder was reluctantly abolished. I was linking them together, the Major and his niece, while at the same time indignantly denying the collusion. Hence the dreams. The idea was growing in me, and I wanted to keep my eyes averted.

I reached the jetty and continued along it till there was nothing before me but the sea. The tide was incoming, running up the harbour in a series of curious, dolphin-like swells. Sun above sea made a gaudy shimmer below a pale, pacific horizon, and a red-funnelled tanker, motoring northwards, showed sharp and distinct as a primitive painting. Where was the dog now, the limping dog? Doubtless the crabs were picking his bones. My slender clue, the other piece of his lead, had not been found by Eyke and his leg-men. Not, for example, in the Major's backyard, where his garage opened on a quiet service-road . . .

I picked up a splinter of driftwood and hurled it into the soft-going tide. Certainly there were holes in the case against the Major – it needed no defence counsel to point them out! He would have to have been lucky, strangely lucky. Nobody had seen Mrs Selly visit him. Of the hundred or more windows overlooking his house, apparently not one had harboured a witness. Had she entered at the rear? Same objection. To reach the service-road she must pass the houses. And if he had gone to the cottage and killed her there, how could he have removed the body unobserved? This last alternative was unlikely for other reasons (of which the tying-up of the dog was one), but one or other we would have to establish if the case was to go forward.

Next, the time factor. Would he have had time enough to commit the crime and dispose of the body? At most, between the time of Mrs Selly's arrival at the house and the return of his wife there could have been no more than two hours. It may well have been less: there was Pamela. Pamela, who'd gone for a spin in her Mini. After their row Pamela might not have come in early, but probably it would still be earlier than eleven p.m. How much earlier? An aching question, and the one that had echoed through my dreams; but (remembering our first interview), I was not ready to accept that she had walked in on the commission of the crime. It didn't fit. What was more likely was her return to an empty house, meaning nothing at the time, but becoming dreadfully comprehensible after Selly had asserted her uncle's guilt. If this were so he'd had less than two hours; but also, if this were so, he was guilty: unless he'd been absent for an unconnected reason which hadn't come to light. Time enough? Perhaps. It depended on the pattern of the event: on the actual killing following very early on Mrs Selly's arrival at the house.

I tossed another grey splinter into the tide-race and watched it begin its journey up the harbour. The pattern of the event: I'd been dodging that issue, wanting equally to establish it and to show it untenable. The latter was easiest. It was clearly implausible that the murder should have taken place in the first few minutes. It would imply malice aforethought, and I couldn't believe the Major was capable of that. There must have been argument and provocation, leading at last to a homicidal row: the Major would be deep into his reserves by the time he was left staring at the limp body. And then, was he so suddenly resourceful? Throwing off the shock of the deed in action? Able immediately to pick up the body, load it in his car and dispose of it? Very convincing! And in addition, during those hurried and terrible moments, he'd have to find time and inclination, both, to strip the corpse and lay it out . . . I grabbed more driftwood and pitched it in. No, the jury would never buy it. But what about me, would I buy it? Knowing, as I did, that such things happened?

Because this was my case, the police case, the case

for the public prosecutor: here was a man with experience of killing, with opportunity and with an overwhelming motive. Yes, the Major did plan his deed. Yes, he was ready for Mrs Selly. He had lured her into the empty house with a promise to come to an agreement. Once she was there he had wasted no time in pointless argument and fulmination: the crime was committed, the body disposed of, and the Major returned home to dissemble innocence. A strong, simple case, and laced with the forensic poison of perversion: whip, ropes and abundant photographs displayed on the table of exhibits. A winning case, oh yes! The defence merely a delaying action. And the truth of the matter? Not my business: I was only the setter-on.

I kicked at the driftwood, scattering shards of it and raising sand and papery seaweed. The bright blandness of the morning had a gaiety that oppressed me. The sun was too immaculate and the blazoned sea too guileless: too much innocence in the shore, the sands, the town with its squat, white lighthouse. What could I do? There was a case to make out. Another outrage on the girl would probably complete it. Crush the Major's feeble offer of an alibi. Impound his car. Invade his house. But yet, yet, if he were innocent – a fool, a pervert, but still innocent – as I must half have thought, heaven help me, when I set him down at the recorder? Because that was the rub: I wasn't convinced. I could still see the innocent version peeping through – or, more accurately, I could see Vivienne, the Vivienne I'd tried so hard to know. And she was wrong, my Vivienne, wasn't the woman who fitted the case: one who'd come back after a rebuff and make good her threats from pure malice. Not her style: she was too abject! My Vivienne would have taken no for an answer. She would never have risen from her knees before Miss Swefling to make a second attempt on the Major. What was the end to be? I'd asked him, and the answer was staring me in the face. She'd been defeated: the Major wouldn't play, and he knew, she knew, the threats were hot air. She'd done for herself. She'd lost the Major along with the girls and everything else. Vivienne was a loser, born a loser; and come to the last throw in the game.

I breathed deeply. This was my judgement. It was based on premises I couldn't prove. 'My Vivienne' was one more ghost I had striven to recall from oblivion. I was like the man who dwelt in the Gobi and who had heard of trees, but never seen one: who had studied books, photographs, prepared specimens, in steppes where not even bushes grew. But for him one day had come an aircraft to carry him to a sight of his subject, when he had exclaimed in astonishment: 'Ah . . . ! So *that's* a tree!' For me, that aircraft would never come: I would never echo: '. . . so *that's* Vivienne!' My steppes were eternal steppes where I had only statements, photographs, prepared specimens. Premises unproven. And leading where, if not to the Major? The broken woman, setting out with her dog, where had her anguish been about to take her?

To Selly?

I stood a little longer with the sealight flashing round me.

Selly?

When I met Eyke later, he had an answer waiting for me on a plate.

He was seated at his desk with a pad before him; and the pad was covered with neat scribble. Also in the office was Detective-Sergeant Campsey, a hefty, untidy-looking young man. They were silent when I walked in. Campsey rose to his feet clumsily. Eyke seemed to come out of a happy reverie: he made to rise, then sat again.

'Sir, I think I'm on to something!'

I put on a poker-face and sat. Judging from his manner, Eyke was being too modest: already he had visions of a case firmly wrapped-up.

'You've been checking with Birmingham?'

'Yes, sir.'

'And Selly has form?'

'Not exactly that.'

'Then what's the excitement?'

'It's just this, sir. I think we've got a motive that'll put him away.'

I grunted. 'What's that?'

'Two hundred and twenty thousand pounds.'

'*How* much?'

'Two hundred and twenty thousand. That's an estimate in round figures.'

I looked at Eyke. He pleasedly stroked a line beneath the scribble on the pad. He'd wanted to amaze me, and he'd succeeded – here was an angle even I hadn't thought of!

'And how does this magnificent sum come into it?'

'It was missing from Aplan, Rayner Co. Ltd.'

'Who?'

'Selly's old firm. That sum couldn't be accounted for when they went broke.'

'And you're saying Selly stole it?'

'Perhaps not the whole sum, sir. But I'm pretty certain he had a finger in it. Especially when you remember his wife worked there too – and she was in accounts for part of the time.'

I rocked my chair. 'I'm glad you're so confident! But it'll take a little more than that to give us a tie-in.'

'Of course sir. But it does sound promising.'

'Just give me the information you got from Birmingham.'

Eyke sat a little stiffer and straightened the pad.

'The firm failed in March two years ago. The failure followed a judgement given against them in a thalido-mide case involving several children. As a result of the Receiver's examination a large deficiency was discov-ered. There was evidence of actuarial manipulation and the illicit conversion of assets.'

'And Selly was suspected of all that?'

'No sir.' Eyke's tone was patient. 'The man the directors tried to put the blame on was their ex-chief accountant, Reginald Aston. He had resigned from the firm a few weeks earlier and then apparently had disappeared. He had sold the house he owned at King's Heath and closed his bank account, leaving no address.'

'I'd say the directors were being logical.'

'But that wasn't how the Fraud Squad saw it, sir. Aston had just lost his wife in an aircrash, and there was evidence to show he had taken it very hard. It seems he'd been talking of chucking-up and making a fresh start abroad, and there was nothing in the books to suggest he knew what was going on.'

'Did they catch up with him?'

'No sir. I don't think they tried very hard. The picture they were getting was of one or two directors milking the funds before the crash came. The chief accountant was a handy scapegoat, but the man they fancied was Joseph Rayner. He was Chairman of the Board and the managing executive.'

'But he wasn't charged.'

'Not enough evidence.'

'In fact they didn't charge anyone.'

Eyke gestured with his pencil. 'A clever job, sir. Some of these people know how to work it.'

'Among which elect you're placing Selly?'

He pinked a little, but didn't waver. 'Yes, sir. I'd say that Selly would be a handy man at converting assets.'

I shook my head; it was fishing too far afield. We would never hang this one on Selly. If the Fraud Squad hadn't as much as suspected him, what chance did we have, two years later? And the odds were long there was nothing in it. Only a fool would trust Selly in a matter so delicate. If the milking of Aplan, Rayner had been successful, it was just because its projectors had been no fools.

'I think we'll forget it.'

Eyke's eyes sparkled. 'Sir, if you'll look at the pattern for a moment—'

'I am looking at it.'

'But if you'll let me go over it! The Fraud Squad didn't know what we know about Selly.'

'We don't know it either.'

'But it's near enough a case, sir, and we'd be justified in looking at it from that angle. And if we're right we can perhaps turn up some evidence that didn't seem important two years ago.'

Well, that was possible. 'All right, then. But remember, it's just an exercise in probabilities.'

'Understood, sir. And the first probability is that Selly wouldn't otherwise have married who he did.'

Silence. I had underestimated Eyke! This was digging into the foundations. All along I had been bothered a little by the incongruity of the match. Now it appeared that Eyke too had quietly brooded over the matter, so that when the occasion arose he could slip it into the argument.

'Go on.'

'Well, she wasn't his sort, sir.' Eyke sounded modestly triumphant. 'She wasn't a raver, she didn't have money, and you couldn't call her a social asset. A fellow like Selly might have given her a whirl but you wouldn't expect him to hitch-up with her – not unless there was a reason that doesn't appear on the surface.'

'Like two hundred and twenty thousand pounds.'

'Like a whack of it, sir, anyway. I'm not trying to say they were in a position to lift the lot on their own. The way I see it is she spotted what was happening and helped Selly to cut himself in, then he was forced to sign her up because of what she had on him. Notice how it all happened at the same time. He married, left the firm, and the firm went bust. And all the time he was flush with money – he paid seven thousand cash for the cottage.'

'You've checked that?'

'Yes sir. Paid cash.'

'He may have got it from the sale of his house in Birmingham.'

'No sir, he didn't. I've got his address there. It was a rented flat in Yardley.'

I nodded: Eyke had been on the war-path. 'Have you run any other check on his finance?'

'Not yet. But I'd be surprised if he's earning the seventy or eighty he was swanking about. Yet he's oozing with money: his clothes, his car, the allowance he was paying his wife. I'd say the signs are there all right if someone wanted to follow them up.'

'But suppose you proved it. Where would that get us?'

'It would get us to Tuesday evening, I reckon, sir. Mrs Selly was fed up with his carryings-on, so she threatened to grass unless he played ball. And Selly wouldn't take it. He'd done with her. He was paying her off till he got his divorce. She may have wanted him back or a split of the cash, but either way he wouldn't wear it.'

'So he killed her.'

'Yes, sir.'

'Where and how?'

Eyke gave me a steady look. 'In his car, sir. He met her on her walk and invited her to drive somewhere quiet for a talk.'

'No.'

'That's how it must have been, sir.'

'That's the way it couldn't have been.'

'But sir, it fits the facts. He didn't have much time

146

for it, so he must have driven her straight on to the Common.'

'And asked her to tie up her dog and undress?'

'Sir, we don't know the dog was tied-up.'

'We know she was naked.'

'But her clothes were with her, sir. It's likeliest that the murderer stripped her at the spot.'

I shook my head very definitely. 'It's not the likeliest for Selly. Selly would have dumped her and got to hell. Selly had an alibi to catch up with. And the dog *was* wearing a lead, and the lead was broken.'

'That could have happened—'

'No, listen! What you've forgotten is the state of the body. It wasn't scratched or bruised, and every fingernail was intact. She didn't struggle, or if she did the killer found some way to prevent it damaging her, and that's not possible in a car unless the victim is in a strait-jacket. Also suffocation in a car is difficult for simple mechanical reasons. Selly would have strangled her, and it wouldn't have mattered to him if she was bashed and bruised in a hundred places. So the car is out. If Selly killed her it would have to be at the cottage, and if you think around that you'll see how improbable it is.'

'But . . . couldn't she have been out of the car when he attacked her?'

'Can you describe how it was done?'

'They could have sat down . . . then he'd throw his coat over her. . .'

'Instead of strangling her – like you and me?'

Eyke's expression was obstinate. 'Well . . . you could be right sir. But villains don't always do what's logical.

If you ask me every murderer is kinky. There's something off-beat about every killing.'

Too true: but I shrugged it aside. 'The point is we don't know how Selly could have done it. And there's this: if he were scared of his wife grassing, why wasn't he scared to walk out on her? He wasn't, and I can give you one reason: to shop him she'd have to shop herself. Nearer the divorce she might have risked something, but until then she'd have sat tight.'

'She'd have got off light, sir.'

'But not off clear. She'd have collected a oncer at least.'

'Perhaps she'd made a deal with him about the allowance.'

'So if she had a deal, why upset it?'

He shook his head glumly, not convinced. As far as Eyke was concerned, it was to be Selly. I could read it in the straight line of his shoulders and the stubborn set of his mouth. And in my pocket I felt the weight of the spool with its seal and the Major's signature across it. Produce it now? I held my hand rigid. The spool was a bomb I was still hoping not to throw.

'Very well – if you want to, go ahead. At least we have some new questions to fire at Selly.'

Eyke nodded at Campsey, who rose lumpishly. We sat in silence and waited for Selly.

And nothing came of that.

Selly strode in bumptiously, his confidence unshaken by our brush on the Common. He was wearing a lightweight suit in a shiny, watered material and a mauve damask shirt with a maroon bow-tie.

He leered at me and at Eyke, then plumped himself on the chair placed for him. He had the air of a man who comes into a room expecting the company to realign around him.

'What's new then – have you pinched the General?'

Eyke's face was magnificently blank. He took a statement-file from a drawer and laid it open on the desk before him.

'I have here your statement, Mr Selly.'

'If you say so I'll believe you.'

'There's a point I would like you to clear up for me.'

'Sock it to me. But keep it clean, squire.'

That was the way it was going to crumble, and I sensed that Eyke could do nothing about it. Selly on form was nobody's push-over: he needed a type of pressuring Eyke didn't possess. A hard-seller. You had to wrong-foot him, keep him continually off-balance. But this was Eyke's picnic: I didn't propose to intervene.

'You say here you had dinner on Tuesday at The Bull in Eastwich in the company of a Mrs Royce.'

'That's it. Jill. No bloody mystery about that.'

'And you were in her company all evening.'

'Give or take a trip to the loo.'

'So if she told us different she would be a liar.'

'She's a liar anyway. What's the odds?'

'In fact Royce tells us she left you at The Bull and didn't see you again until nearly ten p.m. That leaves a period of two hours which your statement doesn't account for.'

Selly's laugh was contemptuous. 'So that's the jack-pot! And of course you'll believe her before me. She's a bloody spare-time pro, mate, didn't they tell you? If you believe her you'll believe anything.'

'Why would she lie to us?'

'I'll tell you why. She has to keep in with the pigs, doesn't she? She'll tell you anything you want to hear if you give her half a hint. But I was with her, don't you worry, and my word's a damn-sight better than hers. So she can get stuffed and so can you. A whore like that doesn't bother me.'

'Is that your answer?'

'Are you kidding?'

'You don't want to amend this statement?'

'Do I hell. It's the bloody truth. I'll swear to what's down there on oath.'

Round to Selly! He was lying, naturally, but the lie was justified by the circumstances. The truth might have been quite innocent, but if he couldn't prove it, it would be no use to him. Worse, it would have meant admitting to a lie, and perhaps have led him into a trap. He showed good judgement in thumping the table and casting aspersions on the witness.

'Is that the lot, mate?'

'No, it isn't.' Eyke closed the file with a modest slap. 'While you're here you can help me with another matter. How long did you know your wife before you married her?'

'Viv . . . ?' You could see Selly's mind work, flashing round the possibilities like a computer. But only a blank card dropped into the tray. 'Might have been a year, or just under.'

'She worked at Aplan, Rayner.'

'Right.'

'What was her job when you met her?'

'Job? She was a typist and general dogsbody round the office.'

'But what department?'

'Orders and Despatch. That's where she was when I met her. Typing up orders and that caper, checking out samples to the reps.'

'Was she doing that job when you married her?'

'Well, a similar sort of thing.'

'What sort of thing?'

'Typing and clerking. Only then they'd shifted her into the Top Office.'

'And what was that?'

'Bloody everything, wasn't it? The Top Office was where the nobs hung out.'

'Was it where the Accounts Department was situated?'

Selly hauled up short: now the drift was clicking with him!

'You're a sweet sonofabitch, aren't you?'

'To put it briefly, your wife worked in Accounts.'

'So if she did what are you trying to make of it?'

'I'd like first to know the name of the man she was working under.'

Selly turned incredulous eyes towards me. 'This joker is bonkers. He's a nut!'

'The name of the head of that department,' Eyke persevered. 'And his position with Aplan, Rayner.'

Selly gazed at him: then he began laughing. It was a raucous, crowing, triumphant laugh. He tilted his black-haired skull back and hurled his quelling laughter at Eyke.

'You b.f.! Do you think Viv was in on it? You think she was mixed up with the fiddle?'

Eyke's mouth was tight. 'I think she was working with a man who was later suspected of embezzlement.'

'You talking of Aston?'

'Of Reginald Aston.'

'Sonny, you don't even have the facts straight. Aston never got a smell of that lovely lolly. He was Joe Rayner's fall-guy, that's who Aston was.'

'But your wife did work with him?'

'She worked for Slater. Slater was boss of the department. Aston never came near the place. He had a posh office along with the brass.'

'And you never met him?'

'Dead right.'

'Your wife never spoke to you of Aston?'

Selly swayed his head. 'How do I get it through to you? It couldn't matter less about bloody Aston. Rayner was the mother-lover who had the money, Rayner and two or three of his cronies. They're a set of double-headed grinding bastards who don't give a frig as long as they're fireproof. They'd flog their grannies for eighteenpence, let alone fiddle funds from a bust business. Ask the dicks over at Brum. They know where the lolly went.'

'So do you it seems.'

Selly rolled his eyes. 'I'm just the boy who ran the errands. Any time you can tie me in with Joe Rayner, I'll confess I'm Jack the Ripper.'

Eyke was through. He took defeat with dignity, but there was no doubt it was defeat. Selly went as bumptiously as he had come and not a drop of sweat on him. Perhaps more bumptiously. It couldn't have escaped him that I took no part in the interrogation, and the reason for that could be only that I was ceasing to regard him as an urgent suspect. Eyke's picnic, designed to put the screw on Selly, had ended by giving him new confidence.

Stiff-faced, Eyke watched him go.

'Perhaps it was too much to hope for, sir,' he conceded.

'At least you tried.'

'I'm not convinced sir. I still think Mrs Selly was a threat to him.'

'But not this sort of threat.'

His chin lifted. 'I'd say it was worth another chat with Birmingham. Castleford too, sir. They should know if he's been throwing his money about.'

I gave up. Eyke wanted Selly, and if faith could do it he was going to have him. I left the office with faith in nothing: just conscious of the weight that bobbed against my thigh.

CHAPTER NINE

I WENT FROM the police station to the High Street, though not with any constructive motive. If Eyke had a hunch, so had I: this case was heading for the files. Or heading for tragedy: one or other. It was never going to finish up in court. That was my strong and depressing conviction as I mingled with the promenaders on Saturday morning.

Nor was there much to cheer me in the High Street. I was witnessing what might well be a critical exodus. A hundred or two visitors, of whom only a few would have been questioned, were in process of dispersing to their four quarters. Cars registered in Leicester, Sheffield, Glasgow, London were slowly threading the crowded way, their roof-racks loaded, their sunburned occupants still wearing the clothes of beach and promenade. Had I been neglectful: should I have insisted on Eyke calling in assistance from Eastwich and elsewhere? I hadn't read the case so, but I could have been wrong: felt now that I was wrong, watching the cars leave. Yet the odds were with me. The caravan site had been the subject of enquiry early on. The other visitors were lodged principally at the north end of the town, and those that were not had come into Eyke's net. Wolmering was small. All the houses bordering the Common and in the neighbourhood of the cottage had by now been covered, and the enquiry was continuing: perhaps one half of the town had already received visits from Eyke's leg-men. The odds were with me . . . but they were odds of logic. And meanwhile I was watching the cars roll.

I watched for the Major: I didn't see him. I didn't see Mrs Rede or Pamela, either. Yet, I felt, normally, all three would be here with their kind on a Saturday morning. Shopping, strolling, chatting, drinking coffee in the Georgian restaurant, buying a *Times* (if it wasn't delivered) or a *Telegraph*, or even a *Guardian*. A morning to enjoy, and a fine one. Why weren't the Redes in the High Street? No red Mini, no shiny Rover with a mouthful of badges and a GB plate . . .

But Selly I saw. Selly stood out like a flea on a plate. He was strutting along with Mrs Bacon, his mauve shirt exposed and garish. An alien: his dress, his strut, his voice all insisted on it: the very set of his head on his shoulders: a Roman come among the Greeks. I watched him from across the street. He stared disparagingly at the passers-by. He peered contemptuously at the shop-windows and made sneering comments in his raw tones. His companion said little: seemed half-embarrassed, half-impressed by his gaucherie; was dressed in a rather-too-young trouser-suit in an uneasy red-and-black contrast. A matched pair? It might be, though I imagined her bank-balance assisted the conjunction. Selly was the peacock. Mrs Bacon's place to hover and admire.

They arrived opposite me, and paused to appraise a display of watercolours in a stationer's window. The display was fresh; from across the street I had been thinking the pictures looked something above average. Not so Selly. I heard his scoffing crow. He jabbed derisive fingers at the display. Across the traffic-murmur I caught such scornful phrases as: pot-boilers, bumf for the mugs. Then a bus slowly passed. Then the scene had changed. A man was standing very close to Selly. It was Reymerston; he was dressed in his fisherman's slop and he had an expression of ferocious composure. He was talking softly. Selly's face was colouring. Selly's eyes were popping, his mouth hanging slack. Mrs Bacon was tugging at Selly's arm, but Selly seemed paralysed, hypnotised by Reymerston. At last, as though he were really a hypnotist, Reymerston snapped his fingers in Selly's face, and Selly, after glaring stupidly for a moment, allowed Mrs Bacon to tow him away. It was delectable. I warmed to Reymerston; I wished only that Eyke had been there to see it . . .

Reymerston saw me, and grinned. I crossed the street. He was still grinning broadly.

'I think I may have lost a customer there! That laddie won't recommend me to his friends.'

'Do you know him?'

'Don't think so. Though his face seemed familiar. Do you?'

'Yes . . . in the way of business.'

'Do you now.' He looked at me shrewdly. 'He wouldn't happen to be the late lamented's husband?'

'He would.'

'Ah . . . I see.' His expression became less flippant. 'Knowing that is knowing a lot. It helps one to understand the poor woman.'

I hesitated, surprised. 'Did you know *her*?'

'Oh yes.' He smiled faintly. 'She tried to seduce me one day, on the beach. Didn't succeed, I may tell you.'

'I would indeed like you to tell me.'

'Would you?' He looked doubtful. 'I don't think you'll find it terribly helpful. It never did get off the beach, you know.'

'All the same I would like to hear about it.'

'Because she might have gone further with someone else?'

'That's the assumption.'

He nodded. 'I accept that. You'd better come back with me and we'll talk it over.'

He gestured down the street. I didn't hesitate, though we were only a few steps from the Pelican. Whether his contribution was important or not, I felt I had earned my interlude with Reymerston. There was a lightness, an immediacy about him: already I was feeling less in the dumps. His long lope fell in with mine and seemed to add spring to my step.

'Do you like doing this job of yours?'

I made a face. 'Not very much.'

'Why do it then?'

'I'm not sure. There's something sacramental about it.'

'Sacramental!' He laughed amusedly. 'I suppose you do hear lots of confessions.'

'My people are usually at the end of their tether. I represent their last link.'

'Through you salvation.'

'In a sort of way. Murder is a crime that must be shriven. The killer puts himself outside society, and I'm his only way back.'

'And that works, does it? He gets back?'

'Well . . . he squares himself with society. The thing is done that can't be undone, but some of the weight gets on my shoulders.'

'He must still feel himself in a special category – officially on file, but still an alien.'

'That is inevitable. Crime punishes itself. But confession renews the forfeited relation.'

'Through you. And that's why you stick it.'

'So I tell myself in times of frustration.'

'And that goes for all policemen?'

'More or less. But we are good and bad too.'

He laughed again. 'But if you're fed up with it, why go on being a crook's confessor? You might be doing something more constructive, something that exercises all your personality.'

'I don't know what it would be. I'm not a painter.'

'Thank heaven – the world's too full of them now. What are your hobbies?'

'Travelling, mostly.'

'Then why not travel. With all your soul.'

I smiled: that certainly was my dream. There were countries that called to me like strange women. To cut my ties and wander through the world would be a fulfilment of my inmost longing. But these were dreams and dreams only, which perhaps would melt with the grasping. Yet it was pleasant just to be reminded of them, to hear them talked of as possible things.

'Does painting satisfy you?'

'If it didn't, I would drop it. I dropped another way of life to paint. I was in business, quite a success. But one day I stopped to take a look at myself.'

'Have you ever regretted it?'

'Never. I was only half-alive before.'

'What I'd want to do would need money.'

'Just decision. The rest will come.'

There was a note of such confidence in that: such a committed belief in adventure. It no longer surprised me that Reymerston should have jumped so casually off the jetty. He had the faith which attracted success because it wasted no strength in contemplating failure. A man good for Everest. But I, myself, had not that faith.

We crossed the High Street at the post-office and continued past the craft-shop. We were over the line. A cluster of red-brick houses sprawled untidily round an open space. Parting them, on the left, was an unpaved lane which bore the name: Fryars Loke. It was short: it ended between blank walls, but with, between them, a glimpse of the Common. Reymerston turned to me with a grin.

'You see, my house is one of the hot-seats. Two of your friends came to see me yesterday. They made me feel a lot guiltier than you do.'

'Inspector Eyke's men?'

'So I presume. The one who grilled me was called Bruisyard.'

'What did you tell them?'

'Nothing at all. I gathered they'd drawn blanks all along.'

I recognised the lane now: it was the one at the top end of the Common boundary; that which divided the terraces of rank and consequence from the cottage and allotments beyond. The cottage was uncompromisingly plebeian: Victorian red-brick, with the mortar in urgent need of repointing. It too faced the lane-end without windows. You went through a gateway into a backyard. Reymerston gestured to it.

'I bought this cheap. A couple of thou. That's peasant's money in this town. Anything else with a Common-frontage would have run me into five figures.'

'Do you intend to restore it?'

'Not just yet. That sort of thing would upset me rather. Besides, I like it looking a bit ruinous – prevents me getting a classified feeling.'

I followed him into the yard. It was just large enough to take a breeze-block garage in one corner. The windows and backdoor had received a lick of paint and also the rails that guarded the worn steps. He ushered me in; and then it was apparent that his casualness didn't extend to the interior. The hall had been meticulously decorated in a cool ivory, and the pemmon floor laid with rush-matting. The place smelt polishy. There was a vase of sweet-peas on the table beside the stairs. A single, large picture that hung opposite was an autumn landscape by J. J. Cotman.

'Come on through.'

We went down the hall to enter a surprisingly spacious front-room. It was in fact two which had been knocked together, along with the bit of hall that had separated them. Mostly a studio, and smelling of linseed. There was a bench, easel, and storage racks at one end. At the other, book-shelves, easy chairs, a stereophonic record-player and a drinks-cabinet. The windows looked out on a tangle of shrubs which almost excluded the view of the Common.

'Too early for a drink?'

'Not today.'

He poured a couple of scotch-and-sodas. We sat down with them by the bookshelves and sipped silently for a while. A place of peace: I didn't want to talk. Through the open windows one could hear larks singing. Reymerston sat sprawling, his legs wide. There was stillness in his pose.

'Shall we get to business, then?'

I sighed. 'When you like.'

'Tell me . . . what are you doing about Major Rede?'

I looked up quickly. Reymerston was watching me with a trace of smile in his eyes.

'What do you know about Major Rede?'

'Enough to suggest you'll be going after him.'

'How do you know that?'

'I have my spies. One, anyway. And she isn't very pleased with you.'

'She! Do you mean Miss Rede?'

He shook his head, eyes still amused. 'Marianne. Marianne Swefling. It so happens we are very good friends.'

'I see.'

'She was here last night. You're not her favourite policeman just now. She had a baddish half-hour with the Rede girl, had to send another teacher home with her.'

'I'm sorry.'

'You can also thank me. I braved her wrath by standing up for you. But I'd still like an answer to my question: what are you doing about Major Rede?'

I looked away. 'I can't talk about that.'

'It's fairly important we should know.'

'Why?'

'There's the kid to think of. Marianne isn't happy about what's happening to her.'

'I'm not happy either.'

'She's not very stable. Now she's convinced her uncle is guilty. Myself, I think that's a load of damned nonsense, but I want to be sure that you think the same. I want your word on it. Something to pass on. To put the kid back on the rails.'

'I'm sorry. I can't do it.'

'Because you think he's guilty?'

'Because I'm still investigating the case.'

'You'll be wrong, you know. He's not your man. We've known the Major longer than you have.'

'That may be so . . . but it isn't quite so simple.'

'A nod. A wink. We'll be discreet.'

'At the moment nothing. I can't help you. Now let's get to this business on the beach.'

Reymerston grimaced. 'Well – I've done my best! But you're a thwarting lot, you officials. And what happened on the beach is mere decoration, a coat of varnish. You know your woman.'

He drank, and I drank. The whisky didn't seem to have much bite in it. He was staring ahead of him, at the books. No flicker of smile in his eyes.

'I rent a beach hut, did you know? Seventy-seven,

near the tea-shack. I go for a dip most afternoons. Swimming has always been my sport. So a few weeks back I began noticing this woman and her dog each afternoon. I didn't know her of course. I'd probably seen her around, but she didn't stand out in a crowd. Yet there was something about her – a sort of heaviness in her look, as though she were absorbing you, calculating your potential; it gave you an odd feeling, it was so unemotional: rather like being observed by a ghost. Anyway she kept coming: playing with the dog, sitting on the beach, taking little strolls; but principally keeping an eye on me, and staring back hard whenever I noticed her. Then she made her move. She brought a ball for the dog. Inevitably, it came in my direction. She'd throw it in the sea for the dog to fetch, but the dog wouldn't follow it through the breakers. Contact made. She told me her name, and began to flatter me about my paintings. She didn't know the first darned thing about painting, but she knew how to use it to establish her come-hitherness. And all the while she kept gazing at me with those big, heavy, expressionless eyes – hypnotic eyes: you felt you could drown in them: fall in and drown. Never once smiled, but with eyes like that she didn't need to. We sat on the beach in front of my hut and she told me about herself. How she'd worked for a firm in Birmingham, married Selly, moved out here. No self-pity, just stating facts. The marriage had never come to anything. Selly had gone off with another woman, but she had the cottage and enough to live on. But that wasn't quite enough, was it? She needed what every woman needed. She was taking

163

the pill, so it was all right, and I wouldn't need to feel an obligation to her. I was alone, just as she was, and the arrangement would suit both of us: a genuine liaison without strings. Certain to be a big success.'

He smiled suddenly, but it was the rueful smile that gave him such a forlorn look. Yet so appealing. Not hard to understand why a Vivienne Selly would make a pass at him.

'Why did you turn her down?'

'I didn't believe her. She was too damned unemotional.'

'Too calculating.'

'Not even that. More as though she didn't believe in herself, either. It should have been romantic, rather touching: the beach, the sun, the rustle of the surf: a woman talking about herself, flattering, offering an open-ended proposition. And she wanted it too, I think. It was all there in her eyes. Yet it wasn't quite real, wasn't going to get acted. She knew it, and so did I.'

'So what happened?'

'I made tea on a primus, and found up some biscuits for the dog.'

I laughed. 'Was it so easy?'

'Absolutely. She wasn't upset. She'd tried, I'd said no, and there we let the matter rest. No fireworks. She drank her tea and told me some more about her husband.'

'Told you what?'

'Oh, about his womanising. Nothing that would help you. Except perhaps the apathy of her attitude – which doesn't surprise me, now I've met him.'

'Did she mention a divorce?'

'She said he would be getting one.'

'Was she apathetic about that?'

'Entirely so. I couldn't have told if she was for it or against it.'

'And you saw no more of her?'

'No. She gave up hanging about the beach. The one or two times I met her in the street, she kindly looked another way.'

In short, another defeat of Vivienne's: with the pattern already harshly familiar. Defeat expected. She was playing a game that didn't have any prizes. It read almost as though she'd played it on purpose, to establish its character of negation. A loser 'doing her thing'. Vivienne not-winning. Proof . . .

I drank quickly, emptying my glass. 'What did Eyke's men ask you?'

Reymerston jerked his head. 'The predictable things. What I saw and heard on Tuesday evening.'

'You were here?'

'Yes. Painting.' He motioned towards the easel with his glass.

'You didn't go to your friend's lecture?'

'No.' He laughed. 'Marianne says I make her nervous.'

'You saw and heard nothing.'

'Nothing interesting. A car passing by was what they were after – latish, probably, after I was in bed – going up the loke here, on to the Common. But that's daft anyway, when you think about it. He'd be drawing attention to himself going out past those houses. If he took the harbour road nobody would notice, and nobody did. Q.E.D.'

'Around nine p.m. you saw nothing of interest?'

'You mean, like a woman with a dog, strolling out there?' He shook his head. 'I wasn't watching. That's where the light comes from: I paint with my back to it.'

'Nothing, then.'

'Sorry. I've given you my little bit.'

I nodded. 'Thank you for that.'

'Wish it could have been more use to you.'

He finished his drink, too, and remained gazing at the books for a few moments. Then his eyes lightened; he grinned at me. 'Do you still have time to spare?'

'Well?'

'I'll show you my paintings. I imagine you'll appreciate them more than friend Selly.'

I grinned back. To hell with the job: I needed a breath of free air.

Paintings.

In a modest way, I claim to have a critic's nose: to smell talent. And I could smell it here, the vigour and grasp of major painting.

Pointillist art. Reymerston was a pointillist. He had taken lessons with Seurat. But not slavish lessons: just the sort of lessons one master accepts from another. His vision was new, dynamic, primitive, using a wider spectrum of tone, in compositions of bended space that filled each canvas with majestic constructions. Seascapes mostly, and landscapes, with one or two fantasies of still-life. All the brilliant image of the coast was strangely captured in Reymerston's paintings.

At first I couldn't tell if I liked it, but I could tell it was forcing a decision upon me. Like it or not, it was adding a dimension of which I could never again be unconscious. A new vision. Reymerston had it: had found a way to transmit it. Working alone here, to my knowledge unknown: his name a cipher to the metropolitan galleries.

'Why haven't you exhibited in London?'

'Do you think I'm ready for that yet?'

'*You're* ready for anything.'

His eyes were doubtful. Yet surely he knew the point he had reached?

'I haven't always been a painter, remember. This is the work of a year or two. Since I gave my whole time to it. I'm not impatient for notoriety.'

'But you need that. You need a public.'

'No. I can still be my own public. I like obscurity. As Lao Tzu said, by not presuming, one can develop one's talent.'

'Only your talent is mature.'

'I'm not convinced of that.'

'Why not ask the question in public?'

He smiled. 'You talk like Marianne! She's always trying to give me a shove.' He slid some pictures away in the racks, then leaned on the racks, his eyes serious. 'But it's not simply a question of my maturity. I'm not convinced of the validity of art, either.'

'Its validity . . . ?'

He nodded. 'Art has been a long time with us. It has had its youth, maturity, its age. Who dare say it is not now senile? Look at the market prices. Already they suggest that painting is a dead art. The work has been done. The masterpieces are counted. We can add no more to the stock. What I do here is painting ghost-pictures, illegitimate visions with no application. It isn't I but art that has lost contact – died: become the key of a lost world.'

'This . . . you believe?'

'Say it's a feeling. The mood I go about my work in. That I'm apocryphal, outside the canon. Painting simply in search of myself. From that point of view my maturity is irrelevant and I have no business with exhibitions. Art has no voice: we're a post-art generation. Perhaps the vacuum has been filled by technology.'

I shook my head blankly. 'But that's just impossible. You couldn't have painted these pictures from such a standpoint. They're not egoistical, and you don't believe they are. Otherwise, why have you bothered to show them to me?'

'Perhaps as a subject for this conversation.' He slanted his face a little, watching me. 'But ignore the logic of it. That's unimportant. What matters, really, is the mood. All art is the product of a mood, and the mood we've fallen into is the mood of inanity. Listen, here's a better set of words. These will tell you more than logic.'

He felt in the hip-pocket of his jeans and brought out a creased notebook. He began reading, but without changing his tone, so that for a moment I didn't realise it was verse.

'Because words in their combinations
Notes, brush-strokes

168

Are infinite, or appear so in the mid-flood of
    creation,
Men, critics
Have thought art inexhaustible,
Are blaming us now for our wilful poverty.

But we were born poor. We are the new
    underprivileged.
Look, look
Our riches are spent.
There Beethoven carved, there Shakespeare,
    da Vinci,
Hewing great empires from the virgin centre.
And we, poor beggars, are left with the
    wrappings,
Cursed, inarticulate, empty, sterile,
Crucified on the lie that art is infinite
Whereas, in truth,
It too has an end.

Pity us, brother.
We are the men we used to be.
We have Shakespeares among us going in
    tatters.
We draw the rags round us, pretending,
    pretending,
Arguing about our millions
As we beg for an alms.
On the little footing the rich have left us
We perform these last few tricks,
Bitter, defensive
At the wrong end of time.'

He closed the book and tossed it on the racks, then sought my eye with his glimmering smile.

'Well?'

'Are these pictures just a last few tricks?'

He laughed. 'You're right. I wouldn't allow that, would I? But the mood moulds them, determines their essence. Because of the mood I'm an alien worker.'

'The mood is decadent. You're aligned against it.'

'Yes – but dare I depend on that alignment being valid? Setting aside the profound feeling that art is completed, and beating a track, still, in the direction of the sun? There is no world now behind me to receive the messages I may relay. The receiver has closed down, is content with tapes of old transmissions. I may be an authentic artist or merely a fool in love with an illusion. I can't know. My point of reference is lost. There is nothing to measure with any longer.'

'You will know *in yourself* how far you've succeeded.'

'But that knowledge exists in a vacuum.'

'So exhibit. Take it out of its vacuum.'

He laughed again. 'It may be extending the illusion.'

'Exhibit,' I said. 'You've gone far enough alone. The mood may turn out to be a chimera. Or you may be the bomb to explode the mood, the catalyst the situation has been waiting for.'

'It's just possible,' he laughed.

'You're a man of decision – at least, you gave me that impression earlier. "The rest will come" – that's what you told me. So why are you vacillating now?'

He shook his head. 'No answer. Except that at this

one point *I am* vacillating. Not for ever, I'm sure: but at this time. As though I sense a great deal is hanging on the throw.'

'Probably it is.'

'So – I vacillate. Even "a man of decision" like me.'

I wasn't satisfied; but before I could begin again we heard a key turn in the outer door. Reymerston glanced at me quizzically: 'That'll be Marianne. I hope she's had time to blow off steam.'

But Marianne hadn't. She entered the room hurriedly, to pull up short: seeing me. Her face flamed, then suddenly was pale, her rich eyes flashing and large.

'You!'

I nodded stiffly.

'I thought you'd be too busy to waste time on pictures.' She moved quickly to Reymerston. 'Andy . . . oh, Andy. The Rede girl has just tried to kill herself.'

CHAPTER TEN

With codeine: about half a small bottle. Sitting in her Mini down at the harbour. While near her the caravan-hirers were packing, and driving by in their laden cars. It was two youngsters who first noticed the lady drooped over the wheel of the Mini, her face flushed, mouth sagging; breath coming in raucous snores. At first they'd stared a bit, expecting that if anything was wrong someone would come along and take care of it, but nobody did; so they told an older boy, who told the harbour-master, who rang the police. Followed squad car and a S.J.A.B. ambulance and a sirening, bell-clanging rush to Eastwich General. She'd live. Eyke brought in the Mini; and the note found propped against the windscreen.

We read it together, that pitiful scrawl, with its hectic writing going all-ways. A confession, no less: a clean breast. In writing that halted and sprawled and trailed as though the mind that made it was already in dissolution. Confession: credible confession. That she'd picked up Vivienne in the Mini. That she'd driven across the Common, suggested love-making, smothered the naked woman with her own clothes. Why? Did the motive matter? If because she knew that Vivienne was blackmailing the Major? If because, after the interview with Miss Swefling, shame had suddenly transmuted itself into violence? Possible, plausible, confessed to, and sealed with a lethal dose of codeine: our case: death resulting from a homicidal attack by a disturbed teenager. At that, she might even get off. Sudden, irresistible impulse of moral revulsion.

I touched the note gently. 'But of course . . . suspect.'

Eyke lifted his head. 'I'm not so sure, sir.'

'Where's the Major?'

'He's gone to the hospital. Mrs Rede too. With Sergeant Campsey.'

'Campsey's waiting there?'

'Yes. But he won't get a word with her just yet.'

'There's no hurry.'

'Not very much, sir. If she never came round, we'd have enough.'

I moved away from the desk, went to stare through the window: at the gravelled yard with its weight of sunlight. Still in my pocket the Major's spool and the tape round it, and the signature. Which was the most suspect – that heavy little disc, or the scrawled paper? Who had been protecting who . . . or were these two sides of a single coin?

'You spoke to Miss Rede on the Wednesday.'

'Yes sir. I took her statement.'

'What was your feeling about her then?'

Eyke hesitated. 'She was a bit defiant.'

'Defiant about what had been going on?'

'That's what she was most concerned about, sir. But I didn't put a lot of pressure on her. I didn't know for certain the girls were mixed up with it.'

'What was her attitude about the death of Mrs Selly?'

Eyke hesitated again. 'Rather quiet.'

'Shocked?'

'She didn't make a lot of fuss. None of them did, if it comes to that.'

'It didn't occur to you then that she might be guilty.'

A longer pause. 'No sir.'

'And certainly not that she was likely to attempt suicide?'

'No sir.' Eyke sounded huffish.

'So what are your comments on that?'

I heard his chair creak slightly behind me. 'Sir, I don't think it is very relevant, not the impression I got when I took her statement.'

'Why isn't it relevant?'

'Because she'd have thought she was in the clear, sir. She'd be acting confident, just like her friends. But that would wear off when we kept going at it, when she realised we were going to get her in the end.'

'What would give her that impression?'

'We didn't arrest Selly.'

'And that was enough to bring about the change?'

'She knew we weren't satisfied. Then you saw her again, sir, which would have given her the idea we were after her.'

I shook my head at the sparrows on the gravel. 'I

can tell you what brought about the change in Miss Rede. It was Selly's putting into her head that her uncle was guilty, and her belief that she had betrayed her uncle to me. I know that's the case. I've been talking to Miss Swefling. She got it out of the girl after I'd questioned her. On the face of it, Pamela Rede confessed and attempted suicide to protect and make restitution to her uncle.'

'On the face of it, sir . . . ?'

I simply shrugged. Another idea had scratched at my brain. Though I wanted to forget it, Marianne Swefling still remained in the area of suspicion. Suppose Pamela Rede had had a third shock: had somehow gathered from Miss Swefling that the latter was guilty. Then the price of undoing the betrayal of her uncle became the alternative betrayal of a, perhaps, much-admired mistress. Out of that, it was easy to believe, such an act and confession might come.

I turned. Eyke was staring hard at me; had read my little moment of doubt. 'On the face of it, sir, I would have thought that this confession sounded very likely. Whatever her motive, Miss Rede had opportunity, and her account of what happened does square with the facts. It goes even further. It explains why we found the body naked and unmarked. In the situation described Mrs Selly may very well have been taken by surprise and have put up no fight.'

'Not even a reflex grab at her assailant?'

'I think it's a credible assumption, sir. The shock, the unexpectedness may have paralysed her, and she lost consciousness without a struggle.'

I grunted. So improbable! Yet something of that

175

sort must have happened. And out of all my much experience, I had been able to suggest nothing more likely.

'What about the dog?'

'Perhaps we've given it too much importance.' Eyke was well-abreast of my wavering confidence. 'The dog may never have entered into it, sir, may have been just an irrelevant incident. The lead could have broken at any time, say when Mrs Selly was walking the dog. It may have seen a cat or another dog and jumped after it, breaking the lead. Then it took off and wouldn't be called back to her. There'd be nothing she could do about that. She'd just have to leave it to find its way home, to come scratching at the door when it was tired of its jaunt.'

True. True. The cottage door was scratched.

'There's nothing in the note that isn't public knowledge.'

'Actually, that's the point I was about to make, sir. The note is convincing, very convincing, but in court it may not stand up.'

'By itself it will never get to court!'

'Exactly what I'm leading up to, sir. As far as we're concerned, this is most likely what happened; but it's a case we're never going to win. There can't be any evidence. We have the car, but whatever it gives us will be inconclusive. It may often have been driven on the Common, and Mrs Selly may often have been given a lift in it. As for the girl, you know the Major. He'll have a solicitor talk to her before we do. And if we did get confirmatory details from her they could be easily discredited in court. She may even be persuaded to retract this confession. And we know where the jury's sympathy will lie.'

I gazed at this man: I had to admire him. 'So in a couple of words, what are you saying?'

'I'm saying sir—' he glanced over his shoulder – 'I'm saying this case is just about over. Of course we'll carry on doing what's necessary, but I feel we should use our discretion about that. And if you don't mind me saying so, sir, I'm pretty sure this is the course that will appeal to the Chief Constable.'

'I'm sure it will. What about the press?'

Eyke stared aslant at his desk-calendar. 'I believe you enjoy a special relationship with them, sir. I was hoping you could help us with that angle.'

He looked back suddenly at me. I made my eyes blank. Yes, this indeed was the case for Wolmering. Near enough. A pity about Selly, but first things first: protect one's own. And for me, wasn't it near enough too, shouldn't I be satisfied with Wolmering's scape-goat – content to let this unhappy business slide into a decent, healing oblivion? Vivienne was dead: no bringing her back. No purpose to be served by perse-cuting the girl. We wouldn't win it, so why proceed with it, exhibiting our official vindictiveness to a hos-tile public? Near enough! All it required was a simple, easy act of faith.

'Only . . . she didn't do it.'

Eyke's eyes glittered. 'In my opinion, sir, she did.'

'In your opinion. But your opinion is prejudiced. And it doesn't take into consideration – this.'

I drew the spool from my pocket. Eyke's eyes switched to it; suddenly gone small. He must have heard I'd had the Major in the office, noticed a spool was missing from the recorder. He said nothing. I reached across and laid the spool on the suicide note. Signatures uppermost. The complete picture. He stared at the spool as though it might sting him.

'I was being discreet too. I took a chance on the Major ratting. But I don't think the Major will – not the way things have turned out.'

'This is . . . proof?'

'A half-dug grave. But now we have to finish the job.'

After a pause, he reached for the spool; but I put his hand aside.

'Wait for the Major.'

A long wait. The Major wouldn't come until his niece was out of danger, had spoken to him. That took time, and neither Eyke nor anybody else intended to rush him. I retired to Saturday lunch at the Pelican, which turned out to be a popular Wolmering function. The Town was there; so was Selly; so was Miss Swefling, squired by Reymerston. Well, a Roman holiday was in the making, and the number of reporters had risen to five: two from Murdoch-country. Later, in the coffee-room, I had the pleasure of enjoying my 'special relation' with them. Then I strolled for a while, feeling unable to sit it out with Eyke in the office; but when I did return, after three, there was yet another hour of waiting to get through. Nothing altered: life at a stand-still, which is the horror that pervades police-stations. Eyke in his chair, the spool on the note: non-time not-passing: the perpetual arrest. In a better world there would be quiet music and perhaps some of Reymerston's pictures, in a police-station.

At ten minutes past four Eyke's phone rang.

'Yes. Bring him straight in.'

Almost immediately the door was thumped heavily and Campsey ushered in the Major. He was dressed in his Saturday tweeds, very well-cut West-of-England, with a crisp shirt of fine linen and a regimental tie. But all that was wasted. The man inside was a mere gesture of his former self. His brisk step had become a shamble, his eyes were glazed and unfocusing. The entire set of his face had disintegrated into something puffy, dragged, broken: almost as though he had suffered a stroke. His monocle hung from its cord unregarded.

And Eyke, he didn't look much happier, as he scrambled to his feet in a sort of ferocious deference. For a second he hesitated, half-up, half-down, mouth drooping, grey eyes wretched.

'There sir . . . please sit down.'

He waved awkwardly to the chair he'd placed ready; not facing the desk, as usage is, but informally, to one side. The Major moved to it and sat. Eyke sank back in his own chair. Campsey took a seat at a small typist's-desk, while I remained near the door: an observer. Eyke's eyes were on the desk.

'Sir . . . I'd like to say how sorry I am.'

The Major nodded mechanically, not turning his head. His breath was coming thickly.

'This must be a sad time for you, sir. I wish we didn't have to bother you. But there are a few things we have to clear up, and I have reason to believe you can assist us.'

179

The Major's breathing snagged. 'Assist you, sir. . . ?' His hand moved ditheringly. 'You're right, sir . . . quite right. I'm the fellow you should be after.'

Eyke's eyes jerked. 'I didn't quite mean that, sir—'

'It's true, sir, true. I'm your fellow.'

'If you will answer one or two questions—'

'I should be behind bars, sir. Not fit to live.'

Eyke was stumped. His eyes flickered helplessly from the Major to the desk, then back to the Major. The Major had relapsed into a vacant stupor, shutting himself off: submerging. His eyes were wide but small-pupilled, seeming to scan dully some vast distance. Eyke grabbed the spool.

'Is this your signature, sir?'

The Major quivered and turned slowly. 'Yes, yes.'

'With your permission, sir, I'll play it back, and ask the Sergeant to make a transcript.'

'Whatever you want.'

'You can refuse, sir. Though this will probably save time.'

'Save time. Yes, that's best. Nothing left to hang about for.'

Eyke fetched the record-player and played the spool: Campsey took it down in shorthand. No surprises. I had given Eyke a resume of the contents before lunch. He had flinched, but held his fire. Perhaps he'd hoped the Major would deny some part of it. Not the Major. He sat listening to his voice without a tremor of reaction, either not noticing or not caring how damning the recital was. When it ended, Eyke sent Campsey to type it up in statement form, then he gave me a meaning look. I followed him out and into the C.I.D. room.

'Sir . . . what the devil are we going to do?'

'Do? We're going after him.'

'But sir, he isn't in a fit condition – we could get anything out of him, now.'

'So bully for us.'

'But is there any point, sir? I mean, if he confesses we'll have to charge him. And that's going to finish him, sir, knock him out. We're going to destroy him, if we go on.'

I drew a very deep breath. 'You're assuming, of course, that the Major will merely be covering for his niece.'

'Yes sir.'

'You won't even consider that she may be covering for him.'

'Yes sir – I have considered it.'

'But you like the other way better.'

'I think the other is the right way, sir. On the balance of evidence. On probabilities.'

'Then you've a long way to go, Inspector.'

Eyke flushed to his ears. His eyes were wild for a moment, his mouth grim. But subordination prevailed. He stood hot and silent, eyes lowered, hands clenching.

'Listen to me. The case against the girl rests entirely on a suicide-confession. We don't know of a motive worth tuppence, and there is no evidence in support. What we do know is she was highly disturbed because she thought she had betrayed her uncle, and that would scarcely have been the case unless she was convinced of her uncle's guilt. And about this she was in the best position to know. She was around loose on Tuesday evening. She had spent the afternoon with Mrs Selly. Her confession is tantamount to an accusation.'

'But, sir—'

'Allow me! In the case of the Major we have a combination of two cogent motives: his own exposure and social ruin, and the moral danger to his niece. Only the removal of Mrs Selly was an answer, and it was an answer in the Major's line of business. With whatever justification the Major has had much experience of killing. In addition, he had opportunity: time, an empty house, an excuse to invite his victim. The Major qualifies as a principal suspect and it is our duty to go after him.'

'But if he's innocent. This will break him!'

'Was he innocent when he entered Mrs Selly's bedroom?'

'That was just a lapse, sir—'

'Then he has the less to fear if it happens to become public.'

Eyke stared agonisedly at me. 'I can't do it, sir. Just somewhere you have to draw a line.'

'If you don't do it, I must.'

'But *you* believe he did it, sir!'

I hunched, let my eyes slide away from him. That was the point! Did I believe it? Along with all the logic I could bring to bear, the neat balances, the summing up? Yes, a little I was believing it, or – let us say – beginning to suspend my disbelief. Seeing it as possible: with the eyes that watched the scribble of the suicide-note forming. Pamela's eyes. Eyes, that on Thursday were the haughty eyes of youthful poise: shattered suddenly on Friday: on Saturday staring into death. Could they have deceived themselves? Would she have acted so on a premise? And if she believed, mustn't I believe, and act as resolutely as she? I believed enough. The picture was coming to me. If it were the true one, that would not surprise me.

'Do you want to opt out?'

He looked at me. 'No, sir. This is my patch. I'm going to handle it.'

'I wouldn't blame you. You have to live here.'

He shook his head. 'It's got to be me.'

'You'd better kick off with a warning.'

'Yes sir.'

'And make absolutely certain he understands it. And perhaps you'd better mention a lawyer to him.'

'Yes sir. Thank you.'

He lifted his chin.

And at that, it wasn't going to be a push-over. A change had come over the Major during our absence. He was sitting straighter, his eyes clearer; the monocle screwed back into one of them. He was going to fight! No need now for Eyke to seek out ways to handle him gently – quite the reverse. If the Major was going to fight, Eyke might have his work cut out to match him. Eyke understood it, too. He was brisk with his warning, told the Major only that he was entitled to a phone-call. The Major spiritedly brushed this aside and fixed a determined stare on Eyke.

'Sir. Before you begin your palava.'

'Yes, sir?' Eyke's voice was carefully neutral.

'I have spoken to my niece. She talks of a letter. I demand a sight of it, sir, before I answer any questions.'

Eyke sent me a look. I hesitated; nodded. Eyke produced the note and handed it to the Major. The Major slewed in his chair, away from Eyke, from me, and read the note slowly, his face invisible. He remained like that for too long, was too still, too quietly-breathing. But when he straightened again his manner was controlled, except for an almost imperceptible tremble.

'This is poppycock. Complete poppycock. Had a word with the girl, so I know. Girl feeling responsible, being hounded by you fellows. Dreams up a fantasy. Tries to act it.'

'She – told you that, sir?'

'Never mind what she told me! Girl in no fit state to answer for herself. But you'll have to answer, sir. Answer for driving her to it. To the Chief Constable. I happen to know him.'

'She suggested no motive for what she did?'

'Haven't I said she wasn't herself, sir?'

'Why she confessed?'

'I have just given the reason, sir. Hounded into it by police harassment.'

Eyke appeared to think about it. 'Yet it does seem strange, sir, when your niece was under no sort of suspicion. That was never at any time suggested to her, either by myself or the Chief Superintendent.'

'What does it matter? She received that impression.'

'But not from anything we said to her, sir.'

'I'm saying she did, sir!'

'But we know she didn't. So why was it necessary for her to confess?'

Now the Major's trembling was more apparent, and the note, which he still held, beginning to flutter.

His little burst of initiative was being wrested from him, was leaking away into Eyke's hands. But a last fling! His eye fell on the note. Before they could stop him, he'd torn it across. Then again and again, with frenetic fury, until Campsey struck the pieces from his hands.

'You shouldn't have done that, sir!'

'You devils! You devils!'

'It'll go against you if there's a trial.'

'That's what I think of it, what I think of you. It's a fix, all of it. A damnable fix!'

He tried to scuffle for the pieces, but Campsey pinned him to the chair. He was gasping and groaning, his breath coming in helpless sobs. They got the pieces. Eyke, grim-faced, placed them in an envelope which he dropped in a drawer. The Major made a howling sound and went limp. Campsey patted his shoulder, then withdrew.

'Not very clever, sir,' Eyke said primly.

The Major moaned. 'It's a fix. A fix.'

'You are saying that your niece didn't write that note?'

He moaned again. 'It's the whip that'll do for me . . .'

Eyke ignored that. He shuffled the sheets of the Major's statement with the waspish neatness of a schoolmaster, coolly read the first sheet, then settled back in his chair.

'Now, sir. Perhaps we can go through your statement.'

'No, sir. No. I refuse to add to it.'

'I see you admit here that Mrs Selly was your

185

mistress. Perhaps you can tell me how much you paid her?'

I should never have underestimated Eyke. With all his modest ways he was a fertile interrogator. He had a nice instinct for the question, the phrase that would expose a raw spot in his subject. He would build for it, too, adding together simple questions that gently raised the pressure: then the key one, quietly spoken, but opening a chasm at the Major's feet. Always thoughtful, slow, economic. The bludgeon wasn't Eyke's weapon. A man like Selly could knock him off his length, but not a man like the Major.

'You say you didn't take Mrs Selly's threats seriously.'

'No sir. I knew she wasn't serious.'

'How much did she want?'

'Well . . . five thousand. But that was a loan, you understand.'

'You couldn't snare that much money.'

'No, I couldn't. It's tied up with my wife's.'

'And your wife would have to be kept in ignorance.'

'Damnation, yes! Isn't that obvious?'

A short pause.

'And Mrs Selly was threatening to talk to your wife, if you didn't help her?'

'But she wasn't serious!'

'Yet she did make the threat?'

The Major's thick breathing. The scuff of Campsey's pencil.

By the end of the first session, the first run through, the Major was beginning to seek refuge in vagueness. He was sweating and mumbling, and the monocle had fallen from his eye long since. Eyke, on the other hand, had begun to lose whatever little reluctance he might still be feeling. He was on the track now, he could smell blood; he was settling in to finish the job. It showed at the interval, during which a tea-tray was fetched in. As though the Major and his troubles had never existed, Eyke had a little chat with Campsey about the holidays. Quite deliberate. You give the subject a whiff of the normal, innocent world beyond his agony, the world now lost to him, and with which he can regain contact only by way of confession, submission, accepted punishment. And meantime he is to understand he is just a case, a bit of business the police are transacting. Not a man. Not a human being. Just a bloody obstacle they want to get rid of. If Eyke was playing it that way, then his mind was already made up.

And so back to the beginning, with an appearance of sweet reason and a promise of despatch.

'Now, sir, we'll just clear up a few details. How much did you say you were paying Mrs Selly?'

The second session was longer; I was timing it. It began with the usual rally. The Major had not yet entirely grasped that answering a question never disposes of it. He was still half-believing that Eyke was rather stupid and couldn't remember what ground they had covered, and that by patient re-affirmation he was hastening the end of the ordeal. I watched that belief die as the minutes of the second session crept by. Slowly the Major's puffy face began to drag and his replies to lose their articulateness. His reactions were lagging. He had to pause at each turn, breathing roughly through his sagged mouth. His pupils were small again, sightless, coming to life only at intervals. Nearing the break? Hard to say. Sometimes the subject will fight you for hours – his condition deteriorating quite early, but his resistance continuing up to complete collapse. Though the Major, of course, had undergone preliminary softening: by me, and by the circumstance of his niece's trying to kill herself.

'How could you have stopped Mrs Selly seeing your wife?'

'. . . Didn't mean that. Wasn't serious.'

'I think she must have been serious. She wanted the money.'

'. . . no. She knew. Wasn't any good.'

'But how could she know?'

'. . . did know.'

'When did your niece learn of your predicament?'

'Never!'

'You saw her confession.'

'No . . . not true. None of that's true.'

Pause: a long pause.

'Why are you so certain your niece is innocent?'

'. . . because . . . it's because . . . !'

'Do you wish to tell us?'

'. . . not true!'

Ah well. The evening was young, and Eyke running into form. Then there'd be Campsey to have a turn, the friendly man who might put in a word for you. And the Major would stagger on between them, his denials weaker at each repetition, till, perhaps sometime in the small hours, paralysis of will would be complete. It was in the pipeline, must happen. They were going to break the Major. And I'd put him there. Set on the dogs. Without a single spit of hard evidence. The expert. Sitting watching. Seeing what I'd reduced this man to.

'If you couldn't pay her the money, how were you going to shut her up?'

'. . . she didn't . . . wasn't . . .'

'Hadn't you better tell us?'

'I . . . no . . . isn't true . . .'

About eight p.m. the phone rang and put an end to that round. The two D.C.s had reported in from their search of the Major's house and car. A fruitless search. All it had produced was a painful encounter with Mrs Rede; she had accompanied them back, and was sitting now in reception, wearing the same puffy, beaten look as her husband. And then there was Pamela in her hospital bed. And overseas somewhere, Pamela's parents. We were really doing well, big men: going for the break and likely to get it.

'Sir, I'm pretty sure now you were right,' Eyke murmured, his eye on the drooping figure in Reception.

I winced. 'Thank you. I'd better have been, hadn't I?'

'Sir?'

'Never mind. Keep right on pitching.'

But I'd had enough: couldn't face another bout of that slaughter in the office. I left abruptly, keeping my hypocritical eyes averted as I hurried through Reception. Out into the clean air and innocent streets, the pale favour of evening sunlight. To be brought up short in a dozen yards by a bull-necked man stepping from a doorway. Selly.

'Get out of my way!'

'No – listen! I've something to tell you.'

My fists were doubling, I couldn't help it; I could feel them sinking in his flabby flesh.

'It's the bleeding Major. You're doing him, aren't you? But you don't know what I bloody know.'

'Stand aside!'

'I'm telling you, sonny. I've got the goods that'll fix him.'

I might have hit him, perhaps ought to have hit him, but there was still a policeman behind those fists. If he really had information about the Major I had to hear it, though it came from the devil. Slowly, I let my fists relax. Selly sneered and edged closer.

'That's better. You've got no call to be high-and-mighty with me, mate.'

'What's your information?'

'Something bloody simple. I wonder you clever-dicks haven't spotted it yet.'

His hand burrowed in his breast pocket and came out with a tatty address-book. He handed it to me. Still visible on the cover was the legend: *With The Compliments of Aplan, Rayner Ltd.*

'Look inside. Page one.'

I flipped it open: page one was an advert. Printed at the top was a list of the members of the board of Aplan, Rayner. At first glance it told me nothing: then I saw what Selly was at. The second name on the list was Reid – and this man, too, had a military title.

'Are you trying to tell me there's a connection?'

'Trying to tell you! It's bloody obvious.'

'Not to me.'

'But it will be, mate, if you'll pin your ears back a

minute. All this ballsing about A & R put me in mind of what Viv once told me – that there was one of them living around here: one of Joe's boys. Said she'd seen him.'

'Who?'

'She didn't say. Maybe never knew his name.'

'And this you've – suddenly – remembered?'

'It's the stinking truth. Do you want to nail this bastard or don't you?'

'Not your way.'

I shoved the book back at him with a fierceness that made him stagger. He swore at me: his breath smelt of whisky. I had to get away from there quickly.

CHAPTER ELEVEN

To get away: and not only from Selly. I wanted to get away from that case. From the beginning it had been a painful business, but now it was ugly: destructive and ugly. And somehow wrong. That's why it was sickening me. In my guts I couldn't believe in it. Yet it had to go on; there was no option. The facts had manoeuvred me into this position.

I walked fast, cutting down the High Street, then by the upper harbour road to the Common. No object – none. Just fuelling my limbs with my self-disgust and frustration. Walked on the Common, across the Common, sweating, mocked by the smell of the gorse: back again towards the urbane town with its square flint tower, its white, dumpy lighthouse. A splendid evening! All sifted sunlight and a few orangey clouds over the sea: elderly couples gently strolling: a couple of black-capped girls on ponies. Innocent, innocent – but to last how long, in the technological chaos growing about it? Wasn't the maggot I had found in Wolmering already the beginning of the destruction to come – and Wolmering itself already a fortress, defensively aligned against the final barbarism? Innocence! What price was innocence? Man is the animal who destroys himself.

I strode on. Down to the harbour. The caravan site and the harbour. Where Pamela had parked by the rusty bollards and the rusty, creaking, deserted ship. Where the sea fretted and destroyed the piles and the fishing-boats rotted from day to day and the black rubbish of dead seaweed was beset by midges where it littered the sand. And this was the evening time again, the hour of Vivienne's last walk. From the jetty's end I could see once more the faint mirage of the Harwich-Hook packet. A great sea-ghost, hull-down, with its passengers gathered in the brightly-lit dining-rooms; Dutchmen, content with their day's business, relaxing, enjoying themselves: going home. Again. As it was on Tuesday. As it would be on other Tuesdays. And the lowered sun yellowing the grey sea just as it had done, in Vivienne's eye. Nothing changed. Nothing acknowledged. So much anguish spent in vain. Including mine, as I walked and walked, rattling the shingle beneath my feet.

Up the beach then, up the footway. Up to the six, cold, iron guns. Wolmering's impotent defence, her brave bluff: her gesture. Pausing there. It was deserted, as usual. Only the sad murmur of the surf from below. Empty windows in the few, grand houses; a vacant chair in the coastguard look-out. I leaned against a gun, the chill, age-polished metal, and stared at the spot where the footway descended: seeing her coming, the lean, Creole-featured woman, with the lead wrapped round her hand, and the dog following her. She who would have been a stranger on Tuesday, but who was no stranger now; with her bleak, drained eyes, her depressed mouth, mechanical step. No, I knew her, Vivienne Selly. Knew the bitterness she was carrying. The dead weight dragging at her breasts which no new dress could take away. A woman in life but close to death, feeling it close, and not unwelcome. She hadn't fought it, didn't want to fight it. Vivienne Selly had been ready to die.

Ready to die . . . yet she hadn't sought it: not in the way of a Pamela Rede. Had she in her own way? Taken a deliberate step that she knew must end as it did? I tried to throw my mind forward, force it to follow Vivienne from there: drive it to seek out the hidden image which, even now, was a mystery to me. How. . . ? Pamela Rede had tried to give an answer, but her frenzied fancy had missed the fact. If Vivienne had died as Pamela had imagined there must have been signs of it on the body. Vivienne would have been preparing for love, not death. She would have struggled, however feebly. Would have clutched at what was smothering her, damaging her nails; have received bruises when the murderer restrained her. But there were no such injuries; not one. Nothing to give the imagination a handhold. For all our medical expert could tell us, Vivienne had simply laid down and died.

I nursed the gun, that elephantine death-maker. Had I just fingered the key of the mystery? It fitted so well, if one could believe it, setting aside medical opinion. She had wanted to die. Then why not? I had read of it happening among primitive people.

Of men giving up the will to live, being robbed of it by witchcraft, or the impact of circumstances. True, the P.M. report had said suffocation, but was auto-suffocation entirely impossible? Wasn't it just credible that a determined person might arrest the act of breathing until death supervened? I let the camera turn again. Vivienne walking past me. Vivienne with the knowledge of death in her eye. Coming to the road. Putting the lead on the dog. Seeking her chapel of trees far away, across the Common. The dog? She'd have tied it up on the way there, perhaps to the railings of the pavilion. Then on alone. Undressing alone. Composing herself. Switching off.

Credible, credible, credible?

No, I knew it wasn't bloody credible.

Just that it fitted.

I struck the gun with my palm, a stupid blow that jarred me painfully.

Not credible! Catching at straws! In one hour, two hours, the Major would break. When the sun had gone: when tinsel lights began to frost the passing traders.

That was what was credible, the way it was developing, realising. And no blame to me. To me the credit. Another conviction under my belt . . .

I heard steps near me: it was Reymerston. He had approached without my noticing him – had probably seen the foolish gesture from which my palm was still tingling. His hair was tousled and damp, and he carried a towel slung round his neck – his face scrubbed and glowing; a sort of sea-aura about him. He gave me that little, doubting smile.

'You don't seem very content with life, maestro.'

'I'm not.'

He came to lean on the gun. 'No . . . perhaps this isn't one of life's great moments.'

'Where is Miss Swefling?'

'I left her in Eastwich. We were over there this afternoon, you know. Marianne is taking it on the chin. Feels she should have talked to the Redes yesterday.'

'She won't talk to them now. That's all finished.'

He nodded. 'Yes, it's all round Wolmering. I had a snack in the Pelican when I came back and heard the gossip. The Major's done for. Then I felt like you. So I went for a swim. Wanted to put some sea between me and Wolmering.'

'Did it work?'

He shrugged. 'What did you do?'

'I went for a walk on the Common.'

'Has that worked?'

'No.' I shook my head and turned up my palm, which was beginning to swell.

Reymerston eyed me. 'You need talking to,' he said. 'And me, I need to talk to someone. But I'm damned if I can stand the bar of the Pelican with all the vultures at their prey. Then again, you're a marked man, and the place is filthy with reporters. Shall we go to my place?'

'Let's do that.'

He lounged off the cannon and we went.

We didn't talk, though, on the way to his house; and from my point of view talk was almost unnecessary. Just being with this man had a relaxing effect, made you feel that a worthwhile perspective was possible. As though indeed he did put sea between you and your problems, bouncing you up to a saner viewpoint: his elasticity of mind communicating itself to shape and detach the chimeras dogging you.

We reached his house and he let us in.

'I'm going to make myself some coffee. Something stronger for you?'

'No, I'll have coffee.'

'Good. I like coffee after a swim.'

I went with him into the kitchen and watched him make coffee in an earthenware jug. I thought he was deliberately keeping silent to allow time for my cannon-striking mood to evaporate. Each of his movements was deft and economical. He paid no attention to my presence at all. In as short a time as it might be done he had a tray set and the coffee brewed.

'Biscuits?'

'No, thank you.'

We went into the studio-lounge, now being lit by the last of the sun: redly. The end with the books was shadowed in a sort of fiery gloom. We settled at that end, the tray between us. My walk had given me a palate for coffee, too. It seemed especially fragrant, so that I even postponed the pipe I'd been looking forward to. Reymerston drank his, deep in the shadows.

'So now there's no doubt about who your man is.'

'Very little, I'm afraid.'

'Yet you don't sound happy. Not confident.'

I grunted into my coffee.

'Are you confident?'

'You know I'm not! If I were, I'd be handling the

job myself. But facts are facts in my business. We're materialists. Like Marx.'

He grinned faintly, acknowledging. 'But I take it your facts are circumstantial. Nothing solid in the way of exhibits that might tie the old lad in. And that's what's fretting you. There's no certainty. You've had to blow him up on trends alone. In fact, you're having to force him to give himself away, and you not being a machine, it's getting you down.'

'But that's not all of it.'

'What's the rest?'

'A feeling in my guts. He didn't do it.'

'You – truly – feel that?'

'I truly feel it. Only we've got him in a trap. And he may confess.'

Reymerston drank sombrely, emptying his cup.

'But if he did that, he'd have to get it right, wouldn't he? I mean, you'll have a fairly clear idea of what happened to the woman, and if he doesn't know that you'll spot it at once . . .'

'That should be the case, but it may not work.'

'Why?'

'Our idea of what happened is not precise.'

'Oh, go on! It was reported in the local. And you must know more about it than they do.'

I nodded. 'But still not enough. Frankly, I don't know quite how it was done. So if the Major's confession is in line with the press report, we may simply have to accept it.'

Reymerston looked serious. 'I see. That is awkward. Couldn't your pathologist give you any clue?'

'No.'

'Then the Major's completely stuck with it?'

'Yes. And I'm stuck with the certainty he didn't do it.'

'What a bitch.' He sucked air through his teeth, then held out his hand for my cup. I passed it. He poured more coffee, the double-comfort of the second cup.

'How is he in a trap, if I'm allowed to know?'

I grunted. 'We'll be releasing it soon to the press. His niece left a note confessing to the crime. That's the cleft we have him in.

'The devil. Could she have done it?'

'Yes. Opportunity. Credible motive.'

'And her too – another feeling in your guts?'

'More, in her case. I wouldn't dare proceed.'

He nodded, sipping. 'You're certainly involved with that family. Now I understand why Marianne wasn't allowed to see her. But if they didn't do it, how about the husband? I wouldn't get feelings in my guts about him.'

I stirred my coffee a few times. 'You appreciate that this is confidential information. Heaven knows I'd like to discuss it, but I must abide by the rules. Obviously, Selly is a suspect, and you can assume we have taken a close look at him. A very, very close look. But that's about all I can say.'

'And he is still running loose. You won't proceed with him either.'

'A fair deduction.'

'So we can cross him off, along with the Major and the girl. Any marginals?'

'Perhaps one.' I glanced to see if this specially

impressed him. Apparently not: it hadn't occurred to him that Miss Swefling might be on the list.

'Just one. Plus an open field of tramps, intruders and stray psychos. Which you'll have covered too.'

'Which we have covered.'

'So as far as we know, nothing there. Thus we've come to this position: the scope of the investigation has been too narrow. Unless your guts are letting you down, you haven't cast the net wide enough yet.'

I groaned. 'Do you think I don't know that?'

'Yes. But have you faced it and tried to act on it?'

I was silent. Perhaps he'd touched something there. I may have let the Major over-dominate my thinking.

'You won't like me quoting Sherlock Holmes to you, but the situation seems to call for it. When you have exhausted the probable answers, then you must consider the improbable ones. Why not try it?'

'Have you any suggestions?'

'A person with weak or non-existent motives.'

'But why should such a person kill her?'

'Stick with the improbable! Have all your murderers had powerful motives? What I'm seeing is a person who is irritated, annoyed, perhaps having a distasteful situation forced upon him. Then he acts not wisely but too well, and suddenly the thing has blown up in his face. Really, an accident. And so no motive that an honest cop would give time-of-day to.'

'Could the person be a woman?'

'Not in my picture. I'm thinking of a man she may have made a pass at.'

'Like you on the beach.'

'Yes, exactly. Use that incident as your starting-point.'

'And then comb all Wolmering?'

'It won't be all Wolmering. You can narrow it down to a group of contacts. Men she'd see regularly in her daily routine, but with whom apparently she had no connection. That's the aspect I'm emphasising: lack of apparent connection. You don't need to look for a compelling motive. Simply a man who she might have approached and placed in the situation we are envisaging.'

'But if there's no connection, how do we identify him?'

'You'll have to fall back on your routines. Statements of movements on Tuesday evening, opportunity and the rest.'

'But even then?'

'Use your guts. I'm sure you'll spot him when you meet him. Some little strangeness or eccentric behaviour – like me, jumping off the jetty.'

He placed his cup on the tray, then sank back again in the shadows. The sun had gone now. The room was in twilight except at the studio end, which caught a little after-glow. The easel stood as it had in the morning, with a cloth shrouding the work in progress. I rose and went to it. Beneath the cloth was the beginning of a seascape, rhythmic, luminous.

'Why did you, in fact, jump off the jetty?'

'I told you, remember? Mixed motives.'

'Yes. But what were they?'

'Those I gave you. Plus some thoughts of suicide. And a need for time.'

I returned down the room. I think he was smiling at me, but the light was too poor to be certain. Facing me, of course: sitting easy and relaxed in one of the two big club-armchairs.

'This is difficult to phrase. To the best of my knowledge, you are a man unconnected with Mrs Selly. You are under no sort of suspicion, nor are you likely to be. Yet I think you are trying to tell me you killed her. Did you?'

'Yes.' He sighed softly. 'I thought you were never going to ask me.'

'Did you need asking?'

He nodded.

'Why?'

'Because I can't prove it. Neither can you.'

I moved away again. There was a chair at the studio end, a cane-bottomed affair with flimsy legs. It was cluttered with books. I shifted them to the picture-racks and sat down, facing the unfinished picture. In the shadows I had left a match flared: Reymerston lighting a cigarette. His handsome face showed once, twice, then became a shape in the darkness.

'You are telling me there is no material proof?'

The cigarette glowed. 'There has been none since Thursday. On Thursday, at the jetty, you could have solved this case. It needed only a touch on my shoulder.'

'You had the other piece of the lead?'

'It was in my pocket. I was about to throw it in the water. But then I saw you. Then the dog. It was the most frightening moment of my life.'

'Did you think I suspected you?'

'I thought you *knew*. I recognised you from your picture in the local. You'd only just arrived: yet here you were, coming unhesitatingly towards me. In some superhuman way you were on to me. Any attempt to evade you would be futile. Then right on cue came that miserable dog with its bit of lead, pointing me out to you.' He paused, drawing smoke. 'How can I describe it? I felt the old superstition had suddenly confounded me. I was the man of blood who couldn't hide, whom even the stones and dumb beasts would betray. I was petrified.'

'Yet you helped me to try to catch the dog.'

'What else could I do, at that moment? I was guilty, it was ringing to the high heaven. All that remained was a decent submission. So I gave you a hand. But the dog fell in, and that part of the proof was missing. Also, it showed the Erinnyes could slip, that perhaps the time of truth was not yet. At least I could delay it: I could take time to think, decide whether I wanted to face it or not. That was my state of mind when I jumped. I had no immediate thought of evading the issue.'

'When had you?'

'Well . . . fairly soon afterwards! A jump in the sea is a great aid to clear thinking. By the time you had stopped shouting and gone for help, I was beginning to realise I might have panicked for nothing.'

'So you let the dog sink.'

'The dog was lost anyway. I could never have got him back to shore. All I had to do was get rid of my piece of lead, which I promptly did. Then the proof was gone.'

I stared hard at the unfinished painting. 'And you've waited till *now* to tell me this?'

'Yes – I had to! Can't you see that? Even now there's a danger you may not believe me.' He stabbed out the cigarette, making the cups clink. 'Try to put yourself in my position. I knew straight away, while I was still in the water, that sooner or later I'd have to tell you about it. That was why I followed you into the coffee-room yesterday. But Major Rede got in first. And it was easy to see, from the way you were handling him, that you had some pretty good grounds for suspicion. So what would you have thought if I'd pitched in then, with a rather strange tale – and no proof? Either that I was trying to take the heat off the Major, or that I was a crackpot after a cheap thrill. And I would have been discredited. It would have been no use now my reiterating my confession. I simply had to wait until you'd rubbed your nose in it, and found your guts didn't agree with your head.'

'Even though it led to the destruction of innocent people?'

'Can you lay that entirely at my door? Is the Major so blameless – and his niece? And don't you share a little of the responsibility? I'll accept mine. I'm appalled by what's happened. I'm guilty of not facing up to it on Thursday. But my silence wasn't what sent you after the Major and Pamela – they'd meddled with pitch, and you saw it on their hands. And you – if your guts are so sensitive, why have you laid the Major's head on the block?'

I moved uneasily on the spindly chair. 'But you're claiming the prime guilt is yours. None of this other would have happened if Vivienne Selly were still alive.'

'But am I guilty? And guilty of what?'

'You have admitted killing Mrs Selly.'

'I know. I did. But what does it mean? That's the question I haven't begun to settle.'

I heard him move rapidly: another cigarette. I kept my face turned to the picture. The flicker of flame picked up the colours. Then they greyed again in the twilight.

'Perhaps I can help you. Isn't your real name Aston?'

The match snapped, was dropped in a saucer.

'Reginald Aston.'

'Late of Aplan, Rayner?'

'Chief Accountant to them for seven years.'

'And Mrs Selly also worked for that firm?'

The cigarette glowed: I could see him smiling. 'You don't disappoint me. You did check up on Selly. Yes, I understand Mrs Selly once worked in my department.'

'You understand?'

'She told me herself. That was what brought her here Tuesday evening. She had an idea it was worth money to me to hide my identity from the police.'

'And wasn't it?'

'None whatever. That was her tragic mistake.'

'You had no connection with the missing money?'

'Oh yes. But nothing provable.' He laughed wryly. 'I'm one of those people who seem able to commit perfect crimes. I planned my first one like a Napoleon. The second just happened, but it was equally foolproof.'

'Where is the money now?'

'In Zurich.'

'You were responsible for the whole amount?'

'A quarter of a million. You have to think big in these days of galloping inflation. I needed to be getting on with my painting and I had no conscience about robbing a firm like Aplan, Rayner. Thalidomide broke them, but it was only one of the products they were recklessly exploiting. I siphoned the funds off in easy stages. The real problem was finding an excuse to resign. Then my wife – who loathed me – had a frightful accident, and there was the solution handed to me. I'd edited the books to point to Joe Rayner – whose back was broad enough, believe me – but being new to crime, I took the added precaution of disappearing and changing my name. Quite needlessly, as it turned out. But it gave ideas to poor Mrs Selly.'

'Could you be so certain that she couldn't betray you?'

'Was there ever a warrant for my arrest?'

'One might have been waiting.'

'But was there?'

I hunched a shoulder. He'd done his work well.

'She couldn't harm me. I made it plain to her, and she didn't argue for long. It was like that time on the beach over again, she wasn't really expecting to turn up trumps. Up to that point, a little sick comedy which should have ended with her trailing off home. Only she didn't, she played another scene. And my God, I wish I knew the reason why.'

He stubbed out his second cigarette, half-smoked. I kept my eyes from him.

'You'd better tell me about it.'

206

'I was painting,' Reymerston said. 'Painting that picture. And you've every reason to sit staring at it. It's all wrapped up with what went on here, a symbolic map of the experience. I'd begun it before she arrived. I continued it during and after the affair. I'll probably destroy it; I don't know. There may be a greater therapy in finishing it.'

He rose and went to the switches by the door. A fluorescent tube lit above me. The picture ignited. Every imaginable colour had been 'pointed' in the fluted swell of the long line of breakers. The sky and the shore were not yet begun, were merely ghosted in with rubs of charcoal. But the sea was near-perfect. You could feel it and smell it, hear the deep roar of its successive plunges.

'I think you'll finish it – given the chance.'

'I don't know if I can bear to let it exist.'

'The conception had nothing to do with Mrs Selly.'

He chucked his head sceptically and returned to his seat.

'The bell rang at about a quarter to nine. She was waiting on the step with her dog. Dressed and made up and heavily scented. My first thought was she'd come to seduce me. But no. She had business to talk, something to do with several years ago. I could pretty well guess what it was, so I let her in. She left her dog tied to the rail.'

'How much did she ask for?'

'Five thousand.'

'And that was to have been a business loan?'

Reymerston checked. 'She'd tried it before, had she?'

I spread my hand. 'You can guess where.'

He shook his head. 'The poor little bitch. And it wouldn't have hurt me to shell out. But she tried to use blackmail, that was what stuck, and I could see she wasn't pinning very many hopes to it. Just a try-on. So that's how I treated it; didn't even lose my temper. And she wept in a quiet, helpless sort of way; no fight at all, simply accepting it. I tried to get rid of her. She ignored me. I offered her a drink. She wouldn't have one. It was completely exasperating. At last I left her in here and went out to the kitchen to make coffee.'

'At what time would that be?'

'Around nine-thirty. I switched on the light as I went out.'

'Where was she sitting?'

'In one of these chairs. But nobody could have seen her from out there.'

He motioned to the windows. Light from the room fell on the wild-run shrubs in the garden. From the room the shrubs hid the view of the Common: ergo, from the Common they hid the view of the room.

'Was she still sitting in the chair when you returned?'

Reymerston hesitated. 'No, she wasn't.'

'Where, then?'

'She wasn't in here at all. I thought for a moment she'd slipped out.'

'But she hadn't?'

'No. I called her name. I heard her calling back, "I'm up here". From upstairs. So I put down the coffee and went upstairs looking for her.' He got up quickly and went to stand at the window. 'She was in the bedroom. My room. Stripped. She'd pulled down the bedclothes and was lying naked on the sheet. Just the electric stove burning, the room lit with a red glow. Her clothes folded and placed on a chair. And her heavy eyes staring at me.' He shuddered.

'What did she say?'

'She didn't speak; she didn't need to. Lying there like a debased Velásquez for me to shut the door and have her. Obscenely: trying to turn me on. Her eyes dead, without expression. Just watching me: feline. It was the eyes that truly shocked me.'

'You felt disgust.'

'More like shock. I've been trying to analyse it ever since. When I walked through that door and saw her, saw her eyes, it seemed to stun me. I was there, yet I wasn't there, as though her eyes were splitting me in two: the presence of myself, in a sort of paralysis, and my physical being: quite separate. Look—' he turned to me appealingly – 'you must have met cases like this before. People have tried to tell you about it. A kind of temporary schizophrenia.'

'Do you mean a black-out?'

'Not a black-out! I remember vividly what happened. Only I couldn't stop it. I was like an automaton, with my real self separate, helpless, watching. And she was doing it to me, that's what I felt; I was a puppet being manipulated. I'm not trying to excuse myself – please believe that! But I need to understand, to make you understand.'

'Tell me the rest.'

He turned from me again. 'The previous day I had bought a new mattress. It came packed in a thick polythene bag, and the bag was still lying on a chest in the bedroom. I got it and went to her. She was lying on her back with her arms straight down beside her. I placed it over her up to her chin and tucked it in underneath her. She didn't resist, in fact she helped me. Perhaps thought it was some sort of kink I had. Then I took the second pillow and placed it over her face and put gentle pressure on it.'

'Didn't she struggle then?'

'Never once. Though of course she was pinioned by the bag. She just moved very slightly, as though making herself comfortable, and after that it was over.'

'How long?'

'Say ten seconds.'

'Are you sure of that?'

He nodded. 'I removed the pillow. I thought she was foxing. I had no clear idea that I'd been killing her. Is heart-failure possible?'

I shook my head. The P.M. report had been specific about the cause of death.

'Yet she died so quickly. So very quickly.'

Yes . . . and why not?

'Just go on.'

He dropped into his chair again, but facing the books, not me. 'I came back down here. I didn't know what to think. For a time, I couldn't believe she was dead. You see, I'd become myself again. The split phase was over directly. And then it was too ludicrous. I hadn't meant to kill her. It was all like some strange game.'

'You went on with your painting?'

'Exactly. As though I'd never been interrupted. Expecting her to come down any minute for a cup of coffee: it was still hot. But she didn't come, so I went back up again, and there she lay, quite dead. So I had to believe it then, though still I couldn't feel I was responsible. Yet it was mine, that responsibility. I could go on painting, but I couldn't dodge it. Though I painted like an angel, there she was: my sin at my door. By then it would be something after eleven. I knew the tide was no use to me. I didn't fancy that, anyway – she wasn't dead yet, in my imagination. It would have to be the Common, the furthest end, which once I'd explored with Marianne. I knew of the little grove. She could lie in that. It seemed a fitting place for the wretched woman. So I painted on till past midnight: the foam of that breaker in the foreground. Then I went up and packed her body in the bag and took it and her clothes down to my car.'

'And the dog – still tied to the rail?'

'Yes. The dog gave me a scare. I'd forgotten him. When I came out with the body, he jumped up and began wagging his tail.'

'No other reaction?'

'None. I think the plastic bag must have fooled him. Rather a stupid dog. He was gone by the time I returned from the Common.'

'What route did you take from here?'

'I drove down the loke and to the harbour road.'

'Not directly on to the Common?'

'I decided against that. It involved driving past the row of villas. Nobody would notice a late car in the streets, but one passing the villas would be unusual. I was quite cool then, judging the risks; the business of disposal was rather matter-of-fact.'

'And you met nobody.'

'Not a soul. There was just me and the car, and her in the boot. I drove off the road at the pavilion and steered as straight as I could for the trees. When I got there I parked the car so the headlights lit up the grove. Then I unloaded her: all shockingly impersonal; I think her nudity had something to do with it. She was stiffening a bit, but her arms were still limp, so I made an attempt to lay her out. The expression on her face was wholly pacific, quite different to what it had been in life. I placed her in the exact centre of the grove with the clothes and the handbag at her head. The bad moment came when I had to leave her. Suddenly, then, I wanted to weep.'

'You returned by the same way?'

He nodded dully. 'I wasn't quite so calm, coming back. But the devil looked after me, as usual, and I got back without incident. Then I had to clear up: the sheet, the pillow-cases, everything and anything she might have touched. I sent the linen to the laundry next day, though in fact there were no emissions from the body. I folded the plastic bag into a small package and sealed it with tape and dropped it from the jetty. The bit of lead I missed until two days later: but you know how I got rid of that.'

'What about the car?'

'Nothing there. She was completely enclosed in the bag.'

'Did you check the underside?'

'Why bother? Heath-rubbish can come from anywhere.' He gave me a long, suddenly anxious look. 'You are believing me, aren't you?'

I stared back. 'Yes, I'm believing you. But you've wiped the slate pretty clean.'

'That doesn't matter if you believe me.'

'But it will matter to the Public Prosecutor.'

'The Public Prosecutor . . . ?'

'He's the man who will ultimately deal with your case.'

Reymerston paused, his eyes steady, curious. 'But there'll be no question of that,' he said.

'I think there will.'

His head shook firmly. 'No. I'm afraid you've misunderstood me. What I've been telling you is for your information and to prevent a miscarriage of justice. That's all. I'm not confessing. Officially, I can be of no assistance.'

I rose from the chair and went to pour myself a cup of the stone-cold coffee. Reymerston watched me. He was quite relaxed: the old, half-wistful smile was in his eyes. I drank the tart, gritty stuff and stared at the books over his head. Expensive books; I noticed a couple that I had on my shelves at home.

'This is your decision, your considered decision?'

He bowed his head. 'Deliberate and considered.'

'It won't be easy for you.'

'I understand that. You can scarcely let the matter drop.'

'We'll be bound to make a thorough investigation. And there's also the matter of the embezzlement. The action we take won't be kept secret. You'll receive attention from the press.'

'Understood.'

'Are you prepared to face it?'

He gave a gentle nod. 'Actually, it won't be so bad as you're suggesting, because neither you nor the press dare take chances. There's no evidence in either case except your hearsay account of our conversation. And remember, I have money behind me. I'm not a safe man to take risks with.'

'But money won't buy off the police.'

'What can they do, without evidence?'

'There's manor law.'

He made a face. 'Honestly, can you see that working in Wolmering? In the first place, Eyke won't want to believe my story. He'd prefer to think I'd pulled a fast one, to save the Major. If *you* believe it, that will do for Eyke, and he'll be grateful to me ever after. Am I wrong?'

I swallowed more bitter coffee. 'Yet perhaps there's one thing you've overlooked.'

'What?'

'That you'll have to live with it. With the knowledge that you're a killer.'

He was silent awhile, his eyes large. Then he looked up at me, suddenly.

'But am I really a killer – is that what happened here? I don't think I shall ever believe it.'

'She died at your hands.'

'She died – yes. But were the hands that killed her mine? I had no intention of it, no awareness. I seemed only a bemused and helpless robot.'

'Are you suggesting she willed it?'

'Would that be impossible?'

'It would make no defence at law.'

214

'But it makes sense here. Perhaps the only sense.'

'Then that's the sense you'll have to live with.'

He sank his head again, slow and heavy. I placed my cup on the tray.

'Where's your phone?'

'In the back lobby.'

He didn't stir as I went out.

When Eyke and Campsey arrived, I left. It was still wanting an hour to midnight. The streets were vacant: Wolmering streets, where scarcely a car passed in five minutes. The lighthouse was beaming its double flash indifferently over the sea and the town, probing unshuttered, uncurtained windows: among them the window of a bedroom at Seacrest.

And it was over. Of that I was sure. Eyke would find nothing he could use at Reymerston's house. He wouldn't look very hard either, and perhaps neither would I, in his place. Over: she had wanted death: had been such a one as we take from the river. Had wanted it and sought it after her fashion. Found it: her only success.

And the blame? Who could one blame? The feckless mother in a Brummagem tenement? Guilty of the vicious outrage of a slap that froze the heart of the little girl? Where did it begin? What was the turning-point? Who had given her the final push? Making of her at last the heavy-eyed woman courting, willing her quick release?

Perhaps nobody: no blame. Nothing you could really pin on anybody. No proof. No material proof. Or none the sea couldn't hold.

I crossed the street near the Pelican and found Selly there, on the watch for me. I could have pushed past him and gone on in, but somehow that wasn't my mood. Not my mood: instead, I waited for him; I could see sweet anger in his face. We met in the shadow by the stationer's shop, the shop that was displaying Reymerston's pictures. His voice was low and choking with anger.

'You stupid so-and-so's – you've let him go!'

'Do you mean Major Rede?'

'You know I do! He was on the bloody hook, and you've let him go.'

'The Major has finished helping our enquiries.'

'Finished my arse! You were set to nail him.'

'We are satisfied he has no connection with the crime.'

'You shit. You bloody know he did it.'

He pushed his face up to mine, eyes big, the whites gleaming. I held still, watching him. I saw the change in his expression.

'There's someone else – is that it?'

'We have received certain information.'

'Shit on that! Have you arrested him?'

I shook my head. 'And we're probably not going to.'

'You're not going to!'

'It is very unlikely. We have no evidence to bring a case. But you can be satisfied that we know the identity of the person who killed your wife.'

'You mean you know – and you're doing eff-all?'

'We are not in a position to bring a case.'

'You bloody prat! Who is he?'

'That is a confidential matter.'

For a second or so I thought he wouldn't rise to it. He stood glaring at me with baffled venom. But I needn't have worried. He grabbed me suddenly by the lapels and backed me violently into the shop-doorway.

'You bastard, you *are* going to tell me!'

It was the moment I had been dreaming of. When he went down he lay quite motionless, except his mouth was working, as though tasting the blood. I wiped my hands and glanced around me. Nobody in the streets to see it. Not that I cared. I waited till he moved, then went my way into the Pelican.